Odysseys

A catalogue record of this book is available from the British Library

First Edition: January 2007

ISBN: 978-1-84375-294-3

To order additional copies of this book please visit:
http://www.upso.co.uk/calmady-hamlyn

Published by: UPSO Ltd
5 Stirling Road, Castleham Business Park,
St Leonards-on-Sea, East Sussex TN38 9NW United Kingdom
Tel: 01424 853349 Fax: 0870 191 3991
Email: info@upso.co.uk   Web: http://www.upso.co.uk

By the same Author

A Small Corner

Engaging the Enemy

Seldom at Sea

An Acceptable Man

As It Happened

House of Thorns

Published by UPSO

The Brotherson

&

No Roses

by

Joan Calmady-Hamlyn

UPSO

The Brotherson

Chapter 1

From the side of Bellator, Sam could look down to the small holding which was her home. She sat quietly on the bay cob, her seat spread on the old flat hunting saddle, her legs hanging at their long length in the stirrups, relaxed, easy, as at home as the minnows in the stream that rushed, chuckling, at the foot of the tor.

Bellacombe Tenement was a longhouse but the shippon side had been converted in her Grandfather's time to make a livingroom and a dairy and the boys' rooms were on top. Sam could see one of her brothers out in the paddock in front of the house, lunging one of the new ponies their father had brought back from market last week.

It was a May morning, very early, chill and slightly misty. Shiny wet cobwebs sprinkled the grass and spanned the gorse bushes. In front of her, rose Hobbator with its funny little circle of stunted trees at the foot. Away, across to her right, beyond the edge of the Moor, she could see the other circles of taller trees that stood to the rear of the big house, Ashgrove, where the Lindells lived. Cris Lindell was eighteen, she knew, two years older than she was and had left his public school last summer but was spending this term at her school, Moorcombe Comprehensive, to upgrade a couple of his examination subjects before going on to university.

The cob stood patiently but was getting cold. Sam took up the reins and they walked on down the sheep track across the coarse turf, down to the busy stream, across it and so to the lane, leading to Bellacombe.

As they entered the yard, Nat, her elder brother, was bringing the sweating pony in and her father had come to the door of the cottage.

"Come on, maid" he said. "Get un in and get to yur breakfast. You'll be late for school."

Sam nodded, dismounting, accepting his words, knowing she had plenty of time to change and eat her breakfast and go down the lane to the main road where the school 'bus would stop for her and two others from across the road.

When she came into the kitchen, her mother was at the stove and Josh, her second brother, was already at the table, eating. Both acknowledged her with a glance as she sat down but nobody spoke. Her mother came to the table with two plates of bacon, egg and sausage and put one in front of Sam, checking her neat uniform skirt and shirt and tie and sitting down herself. On the hot plate two more breakfast dishes waited.

Sam ate hers quickly, spread toast and marmalade and got up, picking up her bulky satchel. It was warm in the kitchen after the early chill up on the Moor but when she went out, pulling on her blazer, the sun was breaking through the mist and promising a warm day. A lovely Spring day, people would call it, those people who thought Spring went on until three days before Mid-summer. But Sam dated her seasons the old way and for her Summer had started on the first day of May.

The two other girls, sisters from the Lodge on the corner of the side road that ran down to the village, joined her at the picking-up point for the school 'bus. Sam watched the side road, wondering if Cris Lindell would be coming up it in his little MG but decided that it would be too early, he would travel so much faster than the 'bus which still had to stop at several other picking-up points. She looked back up the lane towards the Moor recalling her ride up there that morning. Linda and Sarah Pearce were talking about some boy they had met at a disco in Lydston Village Hall the previous night and Sam was glad to climb on the 'bus and take a seat away from them.

It was not that she didn't like nor get on with them but they were village girls and she lived on the Moor and did not seem to belong. Nor did she mind that they called her Gyp or Gyppo though her family were not gypsies. Her great-grandparents, her mother's grandparents had been and had travelled in a caravan but her grandmother lived in a cottage on the edge of Thornwood and it was from her mother that she had her thick, dark hair and dark eyes and warm, brown skin. She was glad that this was her last term at school and she would leave in July and be able to spend all her time riding and breaking-in the ponies her father picked up at the local markets.

Moorcombe Comprehensive was a relatively modern building. A broad road ran from the gates up to the main entrance in the centre part, enclosed by the long wings which stretched down on either side. Diagonal white lines each side provided parking spaces for staff and sixth form pupils' cars.

Cris Lindell, locking his car door and pocketing the keys, watched the group coming up from the Lydston 'bus. Among them was the dark girl they called Gyp, whom he recognized as the daughter of Reuben Lee, one of his father's tenants on the Moor. He had seen her riding up there often, since his return from school and had watched, occasionally, her brothers breaking in ponies, filled with pity for the frightened, bewildered animals. He turned and crossed the road and went into the sixth form wing.

When Sam got back from school, Nat and Josh were in the front paddock with their father. They were, all three of them, solidly-built men, dark, a bit swarthy while she had the leaner, more lightly-built frame of their mother. The brothers were nineteen and twenty; she must have been an after-thought, she reckoned. They were too heavy to ride the ponies so they lunged and long-reined them and then threw their sister up into the saddle. Sometimes, if Reuben Lee picked up a solid cob, one of the boys would ride or they would break him to harness and drive about the lanes in the old dog-cart. They called to Sam, now.

"'Ere, git changed and come and get up on this 'un. Then, after tea - "

Sam paused.

"I'll get up on this 'un 'fore tea" she said. "Then I got homework. There's exams start next week." She turned to the house.

"Just like her Ma" said Reuben, with a sort of resigned pride. Rebecca Lee was mistress of her own home and of her three menfolk. She was at the stove when her daughter came in and greeted her with a nod.

Sam had come in through the door at one end of the central passage. At the further end another door gave on to the garden, mainly vegetables. On the right, the door to the livingroom was open and showed the little-used television set and the stairs up to the boys' bedrooms. The dairy was beyond, on the end of what had been the shippon. On the left was the kitchen which Sam had entered, with a scullery and washroom beyond and the stairs up to her parents' bedroom with her own room beyond. The bathroom was above the passage and had been installed when her grandparents had made the conversion. It was convenient for the size and shape of their family but Sam did not consider this. It was her home, she had her place, she did her homework at the kitchen table after tea usually with her mother sitting by the stove and the men were out or in the other room. That was their life.

She came out to the paddock and approached the pony that Josh held. It was sweating and frightened, rolling its eyes at her, trying to swing away. She wished they could be broken without fear: she was sure it was possible. She spoke softly to it and gentled it with her hands and suddenly felt she did not want her brothers lifting her to the saddle, trying her weight across its back. Hardly realising what she was doing, she said authoritatively "Get back" and putting her foot in the iron, swung up into the saddle and walked off. The paddock gate was easy to open and, amazingly, the pony accepted her body movements to position it and the next moment they were in the lane and trotting up to the moor. She thought 'he's reading my mind, he knows what I want to do as I think it'. The discovery startled and delighted her. She stroked the drying sweat on the pony's neck and crooned happily to it.

They did not go far. Sam was mindful that this was a youngster, unused to even her seven stone on his back. Halfway back down the lane, she slid off and led him the rest of the way, handing him back to Josh and stalking into the house, disregarding the curious looks they gave her.

Nat ventured a tentative remark on her exploits over tea.

"Our maid reckons she'm a proper li'l horse-breaker" he said to Becca. "Just got straight up and marched off to the moor, like."

"Takes after my Grandda', then, she do" said Becca, unconcerned.

"I don't want frightened ponies" said Sam, fiercely. "I'm sure you don't need to scare the wits out of them to break them. They'll go sweeter if they trust you."

Becca, sensing the argument to come, put a stop to it.

"Get on with your tea" she said and her three men obediently addressed themselves to their loaded plates.

Sam took the pony up to the moor again that weekend when she was free of school. She walked him quietly, not taxing him by going up the tors but going along the coarse, short, springy turf at the foot. As they were passing the edge of the tree circle at the bottom of Hobbator, he stopped. Another horse came round the side of the trees and halted. The rider was Crispin Lindell.

"Hullo" he said. "I thought this old fellow had heard something and hoped it wasn't a hobbit from the grove."

"A hobbit?" she said.

"Well - not really. Old Hob was a pagan deity or something, wasn't he? And hobbits come from a book."

"I knew about Hob" she said "But not hobbits. I like your horse. What is he called?"

We call him Harry - he's Hereward the Wake for posh. That's a good pony. Nice and steady for a youngster."

"He's only been broken three days." She found herself telling him of her sudden inspiration to get on the pony. "I hate the way they shout at them and threaten them to make them pull back and learn they can't get away. It shouldn't be necessary if you handle 'em gentle from the start."

"That's an old-fashioned way, isn't it?" he said. "This 'pulling back' business."

"I dunno. Gran's Da was a whisperer. She said he just whispered to un and they'd follow him anywhere."

"Perhaps you've got his gift" said Cris. "Well - I must get on. Harry's a bit hot and I don't want him standing."

Sam nodded goodbye and went round the wood in order to make the turn and head back home. She wondered what it would be like to have a horse like Harry and be able to keep him and train him and school him and really get to know him. She had no illusions about the pony she rode now. He would be sold to the first person who inquired for a pony of that type and was willing to pay the right price; or he would go back to the market as a made pony. She had the old cob, of course, they'd had him for some years because the boys used him to round up their stock on the moor. But even he was likely to go if some person wanted to purchase him. She thought she might ask her father if he would find her a horse of her own to break and bring on and perhaps take to shows - after she left school.

So many things were going to happen after she left school. So much hinged on that illusory time. Its reality had not yet really struck her. She would be able to go to the market with her Da, she would really work on the ponies and pick out and show - or show jump - the promising ones. At the back of her mind was the thought that she might get married but the groom was as illusory as the days after the end of school. But he had to have horses and live or the moor. Her dreams really centred on her home.

As the term progressed, Sam saw quite a lot of Cris at school. She was in the Upper Fifth which collaborated with the Sixth in a number of activities and, sometimes if they had been kept late on an end of term play rehearsal or some such thing, he drove her home in his little MG two-seater. When, in fond response to her pleas, her Da brought home from market a dark bay, two-year-old filly, she and Crispin had much to talk about. It was to be hers alone, to handle and break and she called it Just My Dream - or Dream, for short. It was three-quarter thoroughbred, one-quarter native pony and about fifteen-one h.h. at that time. She loved it, caressed it, took it for walks on a head-collar and lunge-rein and taught it to lead from the old cob so that she could walk it down to Ashgrove where Cris had an enclosed arena and helped her to bit it and long-rein.

Inbetween times, through June, she had exams. and perhaps her interest in Dream helped her to get through them without too much anxiety. Cris was also taking his two subjects and the need for study and the pressure of exam. days made added bonds.

Celia Lindell watched this blossoming friendship between her only son and the only daughter of one of their small-holding tenants without comment She could see the promise of beauty in the girl but she could also see that Cris was not yet aware of it. She thought they would be leaving school in July and Cris would probably spend a holiday with one of his old public school friends and then, in October, he would be away to university. There seemed to be no cause to interfere, as yet. John, her husband, aware that anything beyond a common interest in horses was out of the question, typically put the matter out of his mind.

Chapter 2

The end of term, the end of schooldays, when it arrived, came as a bit of an anticlimax. Nothing had changed except the necessity to go to school and that happened every holiday, anyway. That the necessity had gone forever had not yet become reality.

Cris, as his mother had expected, went to stay with the family of his best friend from college and Sam put Dream out to grass, to grow and develop for a year until she was ready for breaking. There would just be one further bit of education and that would be the two-year-old in-hand class at Moorcombe Agricultural Show in August. Cris should be back for that - and for the exam. results too, at about the same time.

Sam was in the vegetable patch at the back of the cottage, digging some early potatoes for dinner when she saw Josh and Linda Pearce walking down the lane from the main road. Reuben and Nat had gone into market and Becca was in the kitchen. Picking up potatoes from the root she had dug and tossing them into a bucket, Sam eyed the pair speculatively. Josh would get a shock, she thought, if he tried anything on with Linda who was well-known at school to be very experienced in what one of the teachers described as carnal knowledge. Sam added a large cabbage to the bucket and took it indoors.

It was a rather heavy July day, not enough for thunder but making for lethargy. After preparing the vegetables for her mother who was making a cottage pie for the midday dinner, Sam wandered outside again. There was no sign of her brother and the girl and she walked over to the barn, entering silently to find what she had expected. The sight of the girl laid out on the straw, her face red and blank and her eyes upturned and, on top of her, Josh's white half-moons rising and falling with his energetic thrustings did not shock her but roused only a faint feeling of derision. She withdrew again silently and hoped that Linda had enough knowledge not to land Josh with parental responsibilities. She did not say anything to her mother.

Nat came back in the old Daihatsu just before one o'clock.

"Da's stopped off at the pub" he said and sat down to his dinner. Becca returned the remains of the pie to the Rayburn.

"There's a jumble sale over to Lydston" Sam said to her mother when they had washed up. "Want to walk over?"

"No, lover, you go" said Becca. "My feet want this afternoon to be quiet. Your Da won't be back yet."

Sam went to her room and selected a couple of fifty pence pieces from her carefully-hidden pocket money. She reckoned that would be enough to squander in the Parish Hall - in aid of the Church - on some bit of finery and perhaps a bit of bought cake and a cup of tea. The 'bought cake' would be different from the home-made by her mother though likely to be home-made by one of the village women and the finery not necessarily for herself but perhaps a bright apron for Becca.

She had on jeans and a thin shirt and sandals and walked without haste up the lane to the main road and turned to her left along it to the turning down to Lydston village.

It was a pleasant little village lined on either side of its one main road with granite built cottages. It boasted the remains - buried - of a Saxon village and a ruined Norman castle. The present day buildings of importance were the Inn and the Village hall, midway along the main street and the Saxon-Norman church at the far end, beside the pub. A rather imposing coach house hidden by some modern lock-up garages suggested that the old Rectory had housed clerics of some note but this was not within Sam's consideration.

Although the bazaar at the Hall had only just opened, it was already crowded and Sam thought she had been sensible to get there so promptly if she wished to find anything left, worth buying.

She had looked at the white elephant stall and considered a white pottery dog for 10p. and the jams and bottled fruit stall, deciding that her mother made enough of those and passed on to the jumble stall where people were turning over the clothes, shoes, scarves and bits and bobs when somebody pulled out The Dress. It was scarlet, silky, shiny, provocative, tempting, alluring, wicked, naughty, couldn't possibly be her size and the pencilled ticket on it said 50p. Sam passed on hurriedly while the other shopper-for-bargains held the garment up judicially.

A cup of coffee and a piece of fruitcake split one of the 50p. pieces in half and Sam slowly made her way round the rest of the stalls and back to the jumble. It was still there, lying in an abandoned pose across a pile of blouses, strident, blazing and just her size. She put a hand on it and held out her 50p.

"It will suit you, my lover, being so dark" said the cheerful woman behind the stall as she swiftly folded the frock and slipped it into a large plastic carrier bag marked

Gateway. Sam smiled, speechless and took the bag, turning away to the door.

School speech-day, when old pupils returned for Reunion, the village fete, perhaps an Open Day at Ashgrove, a Pony Club party - and at all of them Cris Lindell gazing admiringly at a slim figure in a dashing red dress.

Fifty pence for a frock she might never have the opportunity to wear. What were Da and Ma going to say when they saw it? How Nat and Josh would jeer. She didn't care - she could jeer back at Josh and his goings-on in the barn.

She need not show it to anyone, anyway, not till the time came to dress up in it and loosen her hair from its tight pony-tail and go off to the ball like Cinderella. It was so silky and small she could fold up the bag and pretend she had taken it for possible purchases but had bought nothing. She cut off down the village street and decided to go through the woods rather than back along the road.

It was cooler in the woods, shaded from the sun and there seemed to be a little breeze stirring the heavy air. It was very silent and she thought there could be a coming storm. Through a clearing in the trees ran a little stream, breaking the silence with its soft rippling over the stony bed. Here there was a pool, three or four feet deep where some freak of current had eroded the stony bottom, close to the bank.

Sam sat down on the grass. Sitting made her feel hotter and she thought it would be lovely to have a dip. No-one was likely to come through the wood at this time in the afternoon. She stripped off, quickly.

Just as she was about to step into the pool, she caught sight of her ripply reflection and wondered what the frock would look like if she slipped it on. She pulled it out of the bag and on over her naked body. It felt cool and slinky and she dragged the elastic hair band from her pony-tail and thrust it with her shirt and jeans into the big plastic bag, shaking her dark hair free about her shoulders and stepping lightly, dancingly, along the bank, trying to catch glimpses of herself in the water.

Then a voice spoke behind her.

"And what's a pretty maid like you doin' all on her own in the woods?"

It was rough, slurred and much the worse for drink but she recognized her father's voice and turned, smiling. But with the shock and her disinclination for him to see what she had bought, her smile was ingratiating and far more provocative than she realised.

Reuben, seeing a woman in a scarlet frock with her hair flying loose about her face, smiling an invitation at him, did not hesitate.

"So that's the way of it, is it?" he growled and dragged her to him, pulling up the frock and finding nothing beneath which made him tear open his flies and bear her to the ground without further ado.

Sam, stricken dumb, could only lie and endure the fierce, tearing entry and the subsequent thrusts in agonised horror. She found her mind visualising her brother's similar action that morning and the scorn she had felt. She realised, panic-stricken, that an excitement was rising in her, that she was losing control, that she was sobbing and panting. Then, with a terrific burst of - something - it was all over, she was lying on the grass, staring at her father through a tangle of her own hair and he was buttoning himself up and glaring at her, almost resentfully.

"Why dint you say you was a virgin, you silly bitch?" he said and lumbered off.

Sam didn't move for a long time. She felt torn, sore, sticky and completely blanked in mind. The red dress, she knew, was ripped and, looking at it she saw it for what it was - a cheap, tawdry garment, fit only for a tart, trying to lure a man. Which was what she had done.

She sat up slowly and pulled the frock off, regarding the stains on it without emotion. She rolled it up and slipped from the bank into the stream, hoping the cold, flowing water would cleanse her and take away some of the filth she felt about her.

She crawled out and used the top of the frock to pad herself dry before she put on her shirt and jeans again. She wondered what to do. Should she go home and face her father with the frock and the enormity of his action? What would it do to her mother? How much was he to blame? She had been dancing on the grass, she had turned and smiled at him, knowing he had been drinking heavily. Almost without conscious thought she took the hair band from the bag and dragged back her hair into its customary pony-tail. Now she was unrecognizable as the dancing siren and so the course of action was set.

She put the frock into the bag, folding it flat as if it were empty and continued on her way home. She did not see anyone when she got there. Her father was probably asleep on the sofa in the livingroom, her mother in the dairy or the garden, her brothers out in the fields. She went to her room and thrust the plastic bag to the back of her clothes cupboard. Clever catch-phrases they had used at school ran through her mind: what is it that once lost can never be regained? Virginity. What can you never do more than once? Lose your virginity. How they had giggled as they capped one another at cleverness.

Sam lay on her bed, curled up - the return to the womb position, had she known about it.

To keep out of her family's way, to avoid her Ma and Da, Sam took to riding the ponies, hard and long. An excellently-trained lot went to the next market with Reuben and Nat. She brought Dream in from the field and groomed and lunged her in preparation for the August show.

By the end of July, Cris was back. He watched her activities without comment beyond saying that she was thinner. He genuinely admired Just my Dream and praised Sam's work on the filly with sincerity.

"Do you really like her?" Sam asked. "She's well-bred. We've got her pedigree."

"Why? Do you want to get rid of her?"

Sam, breaking her heart but filled with a dreadful suspicion, nodded.

"If she does well at the Show, would your father buy her for you?"

"Why?" said Cris again, curiously.

"I don't think I shall have the time to break and school her as she deserves" said Sam. "The ponies are our livelihood..."

"If - I - bought her, would you come and help me with her? I shall probably take a year out before I go to university - providing my A levels are good enough for me to go, of course."

Sam nodded, too choked to speak.

"Well - after the Show you must put a price on her" he said. "Cheer up! She'll still be almost like yours."

Sam smiled bleakly and led the filly to her stable.

By the time of the Show, Sam's suspicion had become certainty. She wondered if Linda Pearce was having similar fears - but Linda, of course, was experienced and probably on the pill. She worked and rode hard, hoping against hope for a miscarriage, making herself stronger and healthier and, of course, her muscles firmer.

Dream won the two-year-old in-hand class and a week later the examination results came through. Sam rode the cob up to Ashgrove House.

"Do you still want to sell your filly?" asked Crispin and

she nodded, unable to speak. He watched her, sympathetically. "Well, no hurry" he said. "How were your exam. results?"

"I got As for English and English literature" she said. "Bs for geography and history and a C for maths."

"All five passed!" he said. "Splendid! I upgraded my passes so Father is going to give me the money to buy Dreamy - if you're quite sure."

"Yes" she said. "I want you to have her. She'll make fifteen-three or sixteen hands and she'll be strong enough to carry you by the time she's four. You're not all that heavy."

"No - she'll carry me. With that touch of native pony she might be the type to event. We'll see how she goes." Crispin turned on to other subjects. He was not sure about Sam's attitude: she was sad at losing the filly, of course, but he felt there was something more behind the sadness. He would have to wait and see if anything transpired.

Chapter 3

With the coming of winter, Sam was able for a while to conceal her thickening figure under loose jerseys and sweatshirts. But only for a little while.

"Well, my lover" said Becca, one evening as they sat by the Rayburn in the kitchen. "Are you going to tell me about it?"

Sam did not pretend to misunderstand.

"There's naught I can tell" she said. "Except I'm four months gone."

Becca looked at her, thoughtfully.

"'Tis too late now" she said "Else your Gran'ma could ha' done something for you. Or - is he someone whose babby you'd want?"

Sam shook her head, violently. She had forgotten her Grandmother's lore. It had never occurred to her to go to the old woman, so sunk had she been in her fear and shame and desperation.

"Can't Gran do something - now?" she asked.

"Would be dangerous for you, now, my maid. Why didn't you tell me, sooner? Did you go with him, willingly?"

"No, Ma - of course not! I di'nt know - till he had me down - "

"Rape? Do you want to charge him?"

"No" Sam said in a stifled whisper. "I - can't - "

Becca's gaze searched her face. Had she grasped the truth, Sam wondered frantically - or was she suspecting Crispin Lindell and thinking Sam would not accuse their landlord's son?

Reuben's memory of the encounter with a provocative virgin in the woods had faded. He had been far gone in drink and but for a faint sense of guilt it could have been a dream fantasy. Certainly he never connected it with his daughter's pregnancy. In fact, his main feeling was of a relieved understanding of an action that had puzzled and hurt him - the giving away of the filly he had bought for her.

Sam had explained it away by saying that she could school her better in Cris's arena and would have a proper loose box for her and a companion in Harry, Cris's gelding, whereas at Bellacombe she could not be turned out with unbroken ponies. She had not said that she had sold her and had put the money away in her post office savings account.

All the same, once he had grasped the reason for her action, Reuben was angry enough to demand who it was who had put her in this situation. But Sam, mute and distressed was sheltered by Becca who would not let him harass her.

Josh was inclined to smirk at her so she reckoned he and Linda were getting away with it but Nat was raging.

"Who done this to you?" he roared. "Jus' tell me and I'll see he don't do it to no'un else ever."

But Sam shook her head and was silent. Crispin had accepted her situation with regret, understanding why she had given up her filly, worried that it was a rape and she would not name the rapist but not pressing her about it. His mother, having assured herself that it had nothing to do with him, hoped it might see the end of their friend-ship and his father took no notice of it whatsoever - it seemed.

Indeed, John Lindell had troubles of his own and just before Christmas, a stroke left him paralysed and helpless. Cris abandoned his university career and entered upon a crash course in estate management at a local agricultural college. Though regretting the cause he was not unhappy with the result. He loved his home and the course gave him free weekends when he could ride Harry and handle Dream - and help his struggling father and interpret his mumbling speech.

Sam, growing heavier in body and spirits, had to give up all riding and spent her time with her mother in the kitchen or in her room, reading and re-reading the books she had collected for her English studies at school and that she got from the travelling library that stopped at the end of the lane. She walked on the moor and, earlier, had walked over to her Gran's at Thornwood but it was five miles there and she soon became too tired for the double journey.

The child was due in April and it was one day in late March that Reuben came in for his dinner in the early afternoon, in much the same state as that in which he had blundered through the woods and seen the woman in red by the stream. Sam, dishing up the vegetables while her mother divided the meat pie, remembered his bleary eyes and thickened voice as he stared balefully at her heavy figure. However, he did not speak until she got up again to clear the plates.

"'Tis time you told us who got this babby on you, maid" he said. "When 'tis born 'e must be made to pay for un."

"I'll make 'im pay for un" muttered Nat.

"Us don't want no violence" retorted his father. "Now, Sam, were it the Lindell boy you'm alwis around, with?"

"No, Da."

"Leave her alone, Rube" said Becca.

"No, us did orter know" said Josh.

"Well, you shan't, then" muttered Sam and put the plates in the sink.

"Reckon it was Lindell's boy" said Reuben, dislodging a shred of meat from a back tooth. "I'll go and see un s'arternoon."

"No, you don't" cried Sam. "I tell you it wasn't him."

"'E'll tell if 'twas" retorted her father.

She stared at him, envisaging the scene at Ashgrove with her father shouting at Cris, Mr. Lindell helpless, Mrs. Lindell horrified. Anxiety, fury, disgust, over-whelmed her. She flung down the oven cloth she had taken up to get the pudding plates from the Rayburn as her pent-up emotions overcame her.

"All right!" she bawled. "All right! Wait and I'll show you! I'll show you - you shall know who raped me!"

She stumbled up the stairs to her room, leaving her mother aghast by the stove, the three men gawping at the table. From the back of her cupboard she dragged the bawdy, torn, stained, scarlet frock and clattered down the stairs again. She stopped, holding it out in both hands before Reuben, spreading it out so that the tears and the stains showed plainly.

"Remember?" she shouted. "Remember, after you'd bin to market, coming through Lydston Woods and seein' me by the stream? Couldn't wait to see who it was, could you? And virgin - as you knew, afterwards."

She saw his face turn a dirty grey colour, saw his staring eyes fixed on the flaming red of the dress with the rips and the dark stains, saw memory come back to him with horror; heard her mother moaning, saw her brothers leap up, shouting. Then lightning ripped through her body, splitting her apart, she felt flooding wetness and, screaming, fell into blackness.

Once, the dark veil was parted by a thin distant wailing,

that of a cat or a new-born baby and a voice said, gruffly 'a little boy' and then the blackness fell again.

When it lifted for the second time, she recognised her Gran's face looking down at her and saw that she was in the small bedroom of the cottage at Thornwood. She felt, vaguely, that all would be all right now and went to sleep.

So, when for the third time she floated up through the mist into full awareness, she was not surprised to see where she was nor to find her Grandmother sitting beside her. "There you are, my lover" said Kezia and held a cup to her lips. "'Tis a long time you'm bin away."

Sam sipped and felt revived.

"Where is he?" she whispered. "Where's the baby?"

"Your Ma took him" said Kezia. "She'll see to un."

Sam nodded, a feeling of relief coming to her. He would be safe with Becca and she felt too tired to see to him, now.

She went on being tired for a long time, just eating and sleeping and trying to smile at Kezia when she came up to the little room and telling the doctor when he came to see her that she just felt tired. She did not question her condition nor the passing time. She knew she had a healing scar on her belly and assumed they had taken the baby out that way.

When she was sitting out in the garden, she had a few visitors - Squire Thorn who owned the cottage and lived in the big house across Stony Gravel Lane and his daughter who was reputed to have healing powers. None of her family from Bellacombe, however, nor Crispin Lindell.

Then, suddenly, one day, she realised that the Spring flowers were well advanced and she asked Kezia what the date was.

"'Twill be May Day tomorrow, my lover" said her Gran.

Sam looked at her, thoughtfully but not really surprised. It seemed a long time since she had screamed her hurt and anger at her father. She did not ask about him. She wondered if she could ever go home. She would have to get a job somewhere. But just now she felt too tired.

"And I shall be Queen of the May" she said.

Kezia came close and looked down at her.

"They took un out by operating" she said, bluntly. "You'm seen the scar. They took your womb as well. To save you. You'll have no more children."

When she was in her room again, Sam looked at herself in the glass on the little chest of drawers. Her hair had been cropped close during her illness and was growing into thick, clustering curls. It was one of the things she had noticed without taking in the implications. She had been very ill, obviously. Had she been operated on in hospital? When had she been discharged, if so? Would she have been sent home, still unconscious? She didn't know - she didn't particularly care. She regarded her thin, white face with the boyish crop and thought what am I now? A major part of her femininity had gone.

"And I shall be Queen of the May" she said aloud again and the tears came, at last. She threw herself on to the bed in a paroxysm of weeping and, after a moment, felt her Gran's arms about her.

She was standing at the gate of the cottage next day when Squire Thorn came riding down his drive and out of his gate, opposite. He came over to her.

"Morning, Sam" he said. "You're looking better."

She nodded.

"I must think of a job" she said.

He looked down at her. He was a man of over sixty now but with the wiry body and lean, brown face that appear ageless. She knew something of his story - that his Grandparents had lived in this cottage and he had inherited 'the sight' and healing powers from his Granny Carloss which he had passed on to his daughter and that his great-grandfather had been called 'Gypsy' Carloss and broke horses up under the Moor just as her father did.

"I lived here with my Grandmother when I was a child" he said. "I slept in the room you have - but the cottage was smaller then."

"Your Mother was married to Squire's son who was lost in the Great War" she said. "I'n't that it, sir?"

He nodded, smiling.

"When you're ready" he said "Come up to the stables and start riding again. If you're going to look for a job, you'll need some practice."

"That 'ud be fine, sir" she said. "Thank you."

He nodded again and took up his reins.

"You know my sister and my daughter. See them - when you're ready."

She watched the horse walk away up the lane and thought about getting her gear over from Bellacombe. No doubt her Gran would see to it - she couldn't go home - not yet.

Towards the end of the month, Sam came into the cottage and found Kezia with a bundle of her clothes. She had been riding and helping out at the Firethorn stables almost every day of the three weeks since Squire Thorn had spoken to her and her muscles were in good order and her body had recovered its taut slimness.

"'Tes time you were moving, maid" said Kezia. "Reckon you'd best be to yur uncle and aunt up near Ringwood in the New Forest. There'm plenty of riding up there and places wi' horses you could get a job tu. I'll give yu the train fare to Salisbury from Exeter."

Sam paused, looking down at the clothes: jeans, shirts, pants, socks, her jodhpur boots and trainers and a canvas holdall to put them in. This, then, was it. She had known that, sometime, she would have to go. She was not sure why but somehow she knew she could not go home. But now that the moment had come she knew what a terrible wrench it would be. To leave the moor, to leave Dream. behind, to be cut off from all things familiar. She wanted to ask if she could see the baby but she knew the answer and she knew how much more difficult it would be to leave him with her mother if she had seen him.

"Tes best, lover" said Kezia, gently. "Till it all blows over - about your Pa and all. Then, mebbe, if yu want, yu can come back."

Sam went up early next morning, to say goodbye to them all at Firethorn before setting off on her journey. She would catch the 'bus to Moorcombe and get the Exeter 'bus from there - so Kezia told her. She had the money for her fares and a bit over and tucked away very safely was the folded banknote that Squire Thorn had given her "for emergencies" he said. "Don't use it unless you're desperate" he had said. "An absolute last resort - to bring you home."

She liked the idea of having such a safety net and determined not to use it until all else had failed. It gave a strange boost to her confidence.

The holdall was not too big and, besides handles, had a carrying strap to sling over the shoulder. She eyed the moor speculatively as she walked towards the 'bus stop and on an impulse turned up to the moorland road and along to one of the lanes giving on to the moor. It was a fine, sunny day and she thought why not make her way in easy stages, perhaps pick up some jobs on the way. She knew Kezia had not written to her brother and sister-in-law knowing they would accept Sam when she arrived so there was no necessity to get there today - or tomorrow - or next week.

At first, the tramp over the coarse-grassed, springy turf was exhilarating. The sound of sheep, of a bird high overhead, a sharp call from a moorland stallion, all urged her on her way. But it was unaccustomed exercise and the bag was not so light now, and she was getting hungry.

She stopped and sat on a broad hillock. Kezia had put some food in the bag, she knew, for her to eat on the train. She pulled the zip and took out the packet and a small carton of orange juice. A glimpse of colour made her look deeper and she saw her Gran had packed a bright full skirt of cotton and an embroidered muslin blouse. So she should remember she was a girl, Sam thought, however incomplete. Then the memories and black thoughts came crowding.

She ate a sandwich and drank thirstily but her hunger had gone. She wrapped the greaseproof paper about the remaining sandwiches and put them back in the bag. She buried the empty carton under a loose tussock and, shouldering the bag, set off again.

To have attempted such a walk so soon after getting through such a serious and traumatic illness was, perhaps, foolish. To start with it took its physical toll. Sometimes she felt light-headed, barely knowing where she was, sometimes the black thoughts and fears swamped her. She plodded on, doggedly, resting when her body cried for it and facing the darkness of her mind with the wildness and beauty of the moor to which she belonged. She slept one night in a farmhouse, helping with the cows to pay for her lodging. Another night, she slept in a barn. When the farmer's wife warned her of the danger for a young girl walking alone in the moor, she laughed. What could happen to her now that had not already been done? Except for murder and, perhaps, death was no matter, anyway.

The third day she dropped down from the moor into a small village in sight of the sea. She had been to the sea before on a school outing and it did not call her. But the village street and some white cottages attracted her and a field behind the pub with some horses grazing gave her an idea. She went into the bar and selected the man she reckoned to be the landlord.

"D'you need a groom for your horses, Mister?" she asked.

He was a big man with a thick moustache but looked at her in a kindly way, taking in her smooth, brown face and dark, short curls.

"Are you lad or lass?" he said. "You all dress similar."

"Lass" she said "But I'm strong."

He leaned on the bar counter and looked round the room

"'Ere, Squire!" he called.

A man in a group by the window turned round. He made an excuse to his companions and walked over to the bar. A horseman's walk, thought Sam, though not too obviously so. A lean man with a dark face, ruggedly handsome and rather sombre eyes.

"You was wanting a girl for your horses" said the landlord. "Lass 'ere wants a job."

The man looked at her.

"How old are you?" he said, abruptly.

"Seventeen - next month" said Sam.

"Worked with horses?"

"My dad's a dealer. I been breaking ponies since I were a li'l tacker."

"O.K. I'll give you a try. Are you hungry?"

Sam nodded.

"Give her something, Joe, while I finish my drink" said 'Squire' and returned to the group by the window.

Half an hour later, a replete Sam was sitting in the front of a Landrover with her prospective employer who told her he was Simon Randall.

"They call me Squire because my family have owned the land around here for generations. Doesn't bring in a lot, though. If you stop, I'll give you thirty quid a week and board and lodging. At that rate you won't be clobbered for income tax. O.K.?"

"O.K." said Sam. "What horses you got?"

"Only three at present. I buy in - cheap - school a bit, take them out hunting or pointing, whatever and sell on. My wife helped but she's just starting a baby so we need someone."

Sam nodded, watching as the landrover turned between gateless pillars into a curving drive that led up to a rather square-looking stone-built house. They skirted the building, going round the side of it and pulling up in what was clearly an old stable yard. The stable block was also granite-built with a cobbled apron, well-swept. Simon Randall got out and Sam hitched her bag over her shoulder and followed suit. They went into the house through a green-painted door which led directly into a big kitchen. A girl was sitting at a long deal table with a cup in front of her and Simon kissed her hair.

"How're you feeling?"

"Not too bad."

"Look - Lissa - this is Sam Lee who wants a job with horses."

Melissa turned in her chair to look at Sam. She was pretty but had the colourless face of one suffering from morning sickness.

"Hullo, Sam" she said. "Have you eaten? I sent Simon to the pub for lunch because I didn't feel like any..."

"Yes, thank you" said Sam. "You'll feel better if you eat. Can I make you some toast?"

"Tea and toast" said Melissa with a wan smile. "Do you know - I think I could! I've got the tea." She got up and put a slice of bread in the toaster. She was still slim, not yet showing her condition and Sam reckoned she was very early into her pregnancy. "Sit down" she said. "I'll show you a room and we'll make up the bed in a minute. How did you meet Simon?"

"She saw Joe's horses behind the pub and came in to see

if he wanted a groom" said Simon. "So he called me. Says her dad's a dealer."

Melissa, a bit taken aback, looked up at him, questioningly, then at Sam.

"Are you a gypsy?" she asked.

"My Gran'ma was" said Sam. "But we're honest. I don't steal."

"Sorry" said Melissa, reddening a little and laughing. "It sounded like that, I suppose. Where have you come from?"

"Other side of Moorcombe. I went to school there, till last year. But I - got ill and Gran gave me the train fare to go to her people in the New Forest. They got caravans. But I decided to walk over the Moor."

"To walk! From Moorcombe? But - are you going on to the New Forest?"

"No. Not now. I reckoned I might as well see if I could get a job on the way as go and live on them till I found one. They're not expecting me and I'll write to Gran to tell her I got one - if I'll do."

Melissa spread her toast rather sparingly and bit into it.

"Come on" she said. "We'll go and make up that bed and then you can go and see the horses with Simon."

The Randalls' life-style, Sam found, was somewhat different to the Lindells'. Perhaps because Ashgrove was run by an older generation. Maybe Melissa and Simon would get better organized when they had a family and had to have a routine. At present, the house got dusted and swept twice a week when a 'daily woman' came up from the village and neither of them was tidy so boots and shoes lay where they had been pulled off and dirty jeans and shirts collected in the laundry-room until Melissa pushed them into the machine. Sam lived 'as family' and ate with them, mainly at the kitchen table and found Melissa an uninventive cook. After a few days she found a vegetable garden looked after by an elderly gardener who came up once a week and probably, she thought, took the produce home. She picked peas and beans and broccoli and made a vegetable hotch-potch to go with some chops and watched Simon devour it with relish.

"Gosh" sighed Melissa, afterwards. "It was nice to eat something cooked by someone else."

So Sam offered to cook whenever Melissa felt like having a free evening and added it to her other duties.

The three horses were totally varied. One had been point-to-pointing through the Spring and was now for sale. The second was show-jumping at local shows and the third was a youngster and just being schooled. Sam rode out on all three of them in turn and found them good hacks and well-behaved with what traffic they met on the quiet roads.

Sometimes, in the early morning, they rode along the beach when it was empty and washed smooth by the ebbing water. The horses loved splashing along in the shallows and sometimes, later in the day, Sam would come down to the beach and sit and watch the restless tide. But it was summer and more and more people were coming to the seaside and Sam preferred it in the early morning solitude.

Living with Simon and Melissa in their own home brought Sam into closer contact than she could have wished. After the day's work and when the supper things had been cleared away, they usually retired to the main sitting-room, a big, barely-furnished room with an unpolished wood floor lightly strewn with odd rugs, with old, deep armchairs and a big, floppy sofa. Simon usually went first to a desk in the window bay to deal with the day's paper-work and Melissa curled in the corner of the sofa with a book or magazine, no knitting or sewing. She'd get the baby clothes if and when it arrived, she said.

"They're very good in Woolworths" she said. "No point

in paying a lot for something that's only going to be worn for a month or two before it's grown out of."

Sam wondered if she would have felt the same if she had seen and known her baby instead of being so ill. She wondered how much of her wages she would be able to send to her mother to help feed and clothe the boy.

Chapter 5

It was inevitable that Sam should fall in love with Simon. His dark, sombre-eyed face and the fact of Lissa's difficult start to her pregnancy so that he was restrained with her suggested a man deprived. Because the two of them did not show their mutual love, it appeared that he was free. Sam's life-style, since she had returned to herself in her Gran's garden in May, had made her strong and healthy. Sometimes when they were together in the stables she would be watching Simon and would feel an echo of that strange excitement that had taken control of her when Reuben had been raping her. It was a feeling she could not understand because it repelled her and made her feel uncomfortable and unclean.

In the next village, at the bottom of an unmade-up lane, was a place occupied by a family named Hawken. Simon called them the gypsies but they weren't - unless of the tinker variety. They were car-breakers and bought and sold lorries and horse-boxes. The son had held a trainer's permit and they had a couple of racehorses but some peccadillo had caused them to be warned off and they took their horses to obscure tracks on the Continent - to France or Belgium, maybe the Channel Islands.

Sam was curled up in one of the deep chairs in the

sitting-room one day just after lunch. The french windows were open on to the terrace which edged the semi-wild garden. There was a view across to sun-lit fields and the woods and a blue sky and warm breeze. It was a languorous lazy day and the feeling of space and freedom created by the big, empty rooms and the casual approach to life as lived by the Randalls made Sam feel very liberated. At home, work had been the thing. Meals came at regular times. Her mother had been very organized, her father saw to it that none of them was idle. Here, except for regular attention to the horses, things were done as and when needed.

Lissa had retired to lie down and Simon had gone with her to see her safely on the bed.

"I hope to God this doesn't last all through the pregnancy" he said, coming into the sitting-room.

"First three months, I think" said Sam, thankful that it had not happened to her.

"A month to go" he muttered. "She wants some things from the village and then I want to see Hawken. Want to come?"

"Yeah - sure. Lissa will be all right on her own?"

"We'll only be an hour. It's a lovely day ... Poor kid ...I wish she could lie out in the garden but she wants to be in the dark."

After a brief call at the village shop, they set off for the Hawken yard, the landrover bumping over the potholes in the lane leading to it. At the entrance to the lane, a wooden sign, the black lettering on the once-white board almost obliterated, proclaimed 'G. Hawken & Son, Haulier & Breaker.' The lane was bordered by untrimmed hedges and the verges were aflame with the reds and pinks and yellows of weeds and wild-flowers. A broken gate, sagging on its hinges, but mercifully propped open, gave on to the yard proper. To the left, tucked back into the hedgerow, was a small cottage, once white-washed. To the right, half-concealed by a litter of dismantled lorry bodies and chassis, was a long run of roof to an obviously more modern building.

Simon halted the landrover midway between the two and he and Sam dismounted from it on either side as a small, squat man emerged from the cottage.

"Arternoon, Squire" he bawled, cheerfully. "What can I do for you?"

He was a rotund little man, wearing a tweed suit and black boots with a small, tweed hat crammed on a round head and a fag-end stuck to his bottom lip. An indeterminate moustache and beard showed but whether they were grown or just the result of a couple of days' omission to shave was questionable

"Hullo, Hawken" said Simon. "This is Sam Lee. She's come to help with my horses."

"Pleased to meet you, my dear" said Hawken and Sam bobbed her head.

"Are you getting any reasonable horse transport?" asked Simon. "I'm after a lorry - in good order - two to three horses. A part-swap for my trailer."

Sam became aware that two more people had come up and were silently standing behind them, a man of about forty and a younger woman.

"We got a nice box coming in tomorrow" said the man. His voice was ingratiating, a street mendicant's voice, thought Sam. "Frankly speaking, Mr. Randall, you'll like it. Three-horse, herring-bone. Rear ramp. Quite a bargain."

Hawken Senior, looking at Sam, introduced them.

"My son, Harry" he said. "My daughter Josie. Sam Lee's working with the horses at Fallowfield."

"How d'ye do" said Harry. "Pity we got nothing to show you today. But come back tomorrow. It should be here by lunchtime."

He was a dark, strongly-built man and his sister a big-boned woman with a mane of dark hair held back by a twisted bandeau. Sam wondered what the mother was like to have got two such children with a little dumpling of a husband.

"Like to see our horses, Sam?" said the girl - or woman since she must have been over thirty.

Sam glanced at Simon who nodded and Josie led her amongst the tangle of box vans and bits and pieces to a wooden bridge over a narrow stream which cut off the yard from the modern building on the right which proved to be a range of four loose-boxes with a barn and tack-room. Over the half-doors of two of them gazed two handsome heads. Whatever the state of the breakers' yard, the stable frontage was clean and swept and the horses looked in peak condition.

"We bin racing them" said Josie, with pride. "Across the Channel...Not much on, now. Ever done any? Point-to-pointing?"

"No" said Sam.

"If you felt like it - we could put you in some flapping races. I'm too heavy now for flat-racing. So's Harry, of course. You'd be a good weight. Seven stone?"

"Seven-four" said Sam. "It would depend on Mr. Randall."

Simon, when she mentioned it to him as they drove away, was furious.

"Flapping races? Not on your life, girl. If you ever wanted to do anything legit. you'd be banned. Don't get mixed up with their racing - they're banned from every course in the country." He reflected for a moment then said suddenly "Can you drive?"

"Yes - but not on the roads. I'm not seventeen - got no licence."

"Damn! Of course not. Well - Lissa will have to be fit to

drive the landrover back if he's got a reasonable box, tomorrow. What's the time? we'll drop in on my Mother."

The senior Mrs. Randall had a cottage quite near to the lane leading to the Hawkens.

"It's quite convenient" remarked Simon. "Harry's always ready to do any bits and pieces for her - split wood, fix the plumbing, whatever."

"But - if they're such rogues..."

"Oh, only with horses. Honest as the day, otherwise - and very respectful!"

Sam reflected on this in silence while Simon parked the Rover on a piece of wasteland off the road beside the cottage. It was a neat little place, cream-washed with green painted woodwork and a profusion of flowers in the tiny front garden. About the same size as her Gran's, Sam reckoned.

The woman who opened the door to them was in her middle fifties with greying hair, a lined face and lively eyes. She was of middle height, middle build and looked as if she were very active. She greeted Sam kindly when told who she was and drew them in to a small sitting-room.

"I love your garden" said Sam, looking around at the furnishings.

The room was white-walled and the chairs chintz-covered in gay floral design. There was some good furniture and it was somehow, indefinably, better than Gran'ma Orchard's. Sam wondered why because her Gran had some decent old furniture, too and it was kept just as bright and polished as this.

"Yes, I adore gardening" said Mrs. Randall. "Unfortunately, I only have the front patch - there's just a yard at the back. Useful for the washing but no flowers."

"You must miss the garden at Fallowfield" said Sam, thinking of its overgrown state.

"Mother used to keep it in splendid order" said Simon.

"How is Lissa?" said Clare Randall. "Can't she do a little?"

"When she's over this morning sickness, I expect she will" said Simon. "At present, she's too flaked out."

"I'll get some tea - would you like some?"

"Lissa's lying down" said Sam, bluntly. "We said we'd only be an hour. Reckon we should get back."

Simon glanced at her, hesitated and agreed.

"Yes, we should. I might be over to look at a horse-box Harry Hawken's getting tomorrow" he said. "I'll look in then, maybe."

"Yes, dear, all right. Give my love to Lissa."

Melissa was up and in the kitchen, making tea when they got back. Wan-faced and dark-eyed, she managed to show interest in their accounts of their visits.

"But how much is a box going to cost?" she asked. "Wouldn't it be better to keep the trailer?"

"If we keep the trailer we shall soon have to have a new landrover to pull it" said Simon. "These things don't last for ever."

"If you don't go to many shows it would be cheaper to hire transport for the day" said Sam.

"I prefer to be independent" said Simon, shortly. "You stay and have tea, Sam. I'm going to start on the mucking-out."

He went out and Lissa looked after him, sadly.

"He's getting fed-up with me" she remarked. "Can't blame him. I'm a bit of a drip, just now."

"Well - he did it" retorted Sam. "If he wants a son he'll have to put up with it. Here, give me the tray."

They went into the big, empty drawing-room and Sam opened the french windows on to the untidy garden.

"I think Mrs. Randall was regretting the loss of her garden" she said.

"I wish she would come back here to live" said Lissa,

wistfully. "But she felt, when we got married, that we ought to have the house on our own."

Sam poured out tea and took some cake.

"But you could easily make the nurseries into a flat for her" she said. "Then she'd be here but you'd still be on your own. It's silly to waste all those rooms. You won't be putting the baby out there if you've not got a nanny."

"No. We're making the dressing-room off our bedroom into a nursery. Sam - what a good idea! I wonder if Simon would agree - and if his Mother would come back." She took a slice of cake and bit into it, her thoughts taken from herself and her queasy state and Sam thought it was despondency rather than her condition that was making her unwell. The size of the house, the neglected gardens, her inability to ride, the coming child – it had all got on top of her.

"I'd better go and help muck out" she said. "There won't be much - they've been out all afternoon."

Simon had almost finished the three loose-boxes.

"Right you are, Samantha" he said. "Just this barrow-load to go to the heap, then we can fetch in the horses."

"I'm not Samantha" she said.

He straightened up, surprised.

"Who are you, then?"

"I'm Samaria" she said and took the handles of the wheelbarrow. "Gran's people were in Hampshire when Ma was small, in the War and she saw these two ships in Southampton. Scythia and Samaria. She liked it so when she had me, she called me that."

"Ships" he repeated. "But also countries. And, surely, Samaria is where the Samaritans came from."

Chapter 6

Sam did not go to the Hawkens' yard the next day nor did Simon come back with the horsebox. He said it was too expensive. But riding past their lane about a week later, she came to the cottage where Mrs. Randall lived and found her in the colourful front garden. She halted the horse.

"Hullo - Sam, isn't it? How are you, my dear?"

"Very well, thank you, Ma'am. Your flowers are lovely. Don't you ever want to come to Fallowfield and do the garden there?"

Mrs. Randall paused, her arms folded on top of her gate.

"Would they like me to? I don't want to interfere."

"I reckon Lissa would be glad if you went back there all the time" Sam said, bluntly. "She' s smothered by the house and the cooking and not feeling well - and the garden getting such a mess."

Mrs. Randall eyed her, thoughtfully.

"I must come over and have a talk with them" she said. "And see how I can help. How is Simon doing with his horse-dealing?"

Sam shrugged.

"Can't do much dealing with three horses" she pointed out. "If he's only going to keep three he doesn't need to employ me really except he feels he must have someone to see to them if Lissa's sick and needs him. Course, if you were there, it 'ud be all right."

Sam rode on after a few minutes, feeling she had planted a useful seedling. That she might be doing herself out of a job she left to fate. She was a little uneasy about her relationship with Simon and felt that if she had to move on it might be as well. With Lissa so often retiring to lie down and never coming out to the stables, she and Simon were too frequently together - watching TV., mucking out, exercising and schooling - and she was aware of desire within herself.

Towards the end of a hot July day, they had just turned the horses out into the field to spend the warm night out there after passing the heat of the day in the stables and had taken up their forks to muck out ready for the morning.

"Mother comes over today" remarked Simon, pausing at the door of the loose-box where Sam was working. "She's going to sell the cottage and come back here. Lissa had a good idea about turning the old nursery wing into a flat for her."

"It will help Lissa - not to have to worry about the garden" said Sam.

"It will help me not to have to worry about Lissa being alone. Not to mention financially." He came in, closer. "I think this was your doing, wasn't it? Our little Samaritan..." His hand was on her hair and involuntarily she turned towards him. "You do like me - quite a bit, Sam, don't you? You're so pretty ... If you knew how difficult it has been not being able to touch Lissa..."

Sam, almost overcome by her need and her desire for him, was in his arms, listening to his words of endearment, experiencing a thrill from his caresses, lifting her face to meet his kisses. Then, suddenly, the throbbing she felt reminded her of the rising excitement that had taken control of her when Reuben was thrusting into her and a complete revulsion made her fight him off. For a moment they stared wildly at each other. Then she turned and fled from the stables.

She ran until she could no longer run and did not know why she ran nor what she ran from. She dropped into a walk, drawing gasping breaths and found she was crossing the fields towards the sea. No-one pursued her.

The beach was virtually deserted at that time: people had gone back for their evening meal, to their hotels and guest houses and caravans. The last stragglers, dragging unwilling children, were mounting the path to the cliff top.

Sam sat down on a rock, staring at the approaching waves, at the coy wavelets that crept up the sand and shrank back again. She had been running from herself, she thought. She had not been afraid of Simon - he would not have forced her. Would she ever know a normal relationship with a man or would this disgust always overcome her? She thought of Cris, she thought of the clean, empty sweep of the moor.

A dreadful yearning for her home, for the ponies, her brothers, for life as it was just as she was leaving school so that nothing of the past year had happened and she could climb on the cob - or Dream - and ride up the lane to the moor and meet Cris riding Harry and perhaps ride down together to the road again.

But that had gone. Nothing could give her back that time again. It was past and done with and she did not know what lay ahead. The tears came to her eyes and slowly rolled down her cheeks. She let them flow, staring at the sea.

Footsteps on the beach. A gentle hand on her shoulder. Simon crouched beside her.

"Sam ... I'm so sorry. I didn't mean to scare you. You know I wouldn't hurt you."

She looked round, not concealing her wet face.

"The sea makes me sad" she said.

"'The melancholy sea washing on the beach...' Yes, sometimes" he said. "But I make you sad. You are adorable, Sam but don't be afraid. I won't do it again."

"I knew you wouldn't hurt me" said Sam. "I ran, because - ." She hesitated, uncertain. Then "Last summer I was raped."

Simon was sitting on the sand, beside her. She heard his sharp intake of breath.

"My poor child" he said, softly. "Then - what - ?"

"I had a baby in April" said Sam. "My Ma took him - I don't know if he's my brother - or my son - " She laughed, a queer little choke. "My Brotherson. It was my Da, you see."

"Your father - raped you - and you had his child?" Simon's voice was soft yet harsh. "You could have him charged."

"No" said Sam, looking into the past. "No, I couldn't. He didn't know it was me. He was drunk ... and I..." She thought of the temptation of her smile as she recognized her father and shook her head and was silent.

Simon did not question her. He got up and put out a hand to pull her to her feet.

"Come on" he said. "It's getting chilly. I've got the landrover up top."

They walked up to the cliff top, slowly, each aware that there was a change in their relationship and climbed into the landrover and went back to the house.

There, Sam minced the remains of a beef joint and put potatoes on to boil. She made a cottage pie and opened a tin of peas to go with it, thinking of the neglected garden and wondering if Mrs. Randall would get vegetables growing for next year. By the time Mrs. Randall was settled in and Lissa was over her morning sickness, Sam decided she would be away on her travels again. She had no desire to see jealousy dawn in Lissa's eyes nor suspicion in Mrs. Randall's, however unjustified.

So, a couple of weeks later, Sam got out her canvas holdall and packed it with her newly washed shirts and jeans and underwear and the new pair of jodhpurs she had bought with her pay and sat down at the table in her bedroom to write to her Grandmother. To tell her she was moving on towards the New Forest and to enclose the £10 note she had been sending weekly - an old one, so that it would not crackle inside the folded letter. Then she took a look around the bright, tidy little room that had been her home for the last six weeks and went to bed.

In the morning she got up early, made herself some breakfast and left the table laid for Simon and Lissa. Mrs. Randall got her own breakfast in the kitchenette of her nursery flat and, for a moment, Sam wondered if she should go up and say goodbye to her. It was Sunday. Lissa was now blooming and she and Simon would be having a lie-in. The horses had been turned out in the fields to enjoy the night and would come in for the day. Nothing needed to be done - except to write a note.

She wrote 'Dear Lissa, You are well now and can help Simon and you have Mrs. Randall to help you. You don't need me any more but I've enjoyed being here. I hope you have a lovely baby. If I come back this way when I go home I'll look in and see how big he is. Love to you all, Sam.'

It was the last week of July, just over a year since that heavy July day when she had gone to the jumble sale at Lydston and bought the garish scarlet frock. But the early morning gave promise of a fine, bright day without threat of thunder; she was seventeen and three weeks old, she had her post office book detailing the deposits of her pay and a driving licence because she had passed the test that Simon had arranged for the day after her birthday. In her pocket was the remainder of her last week's pay and it was the knowledge of her affluence that made her jump on the 'bus that came along the coast road where she had set off walking. Which was why Simon, anxiously scanning the roads leading out of the village, in the landrover, missed her.

Chapter 7

Sam sat down on the bed and looked around. She had dumped her canvas holdall on the floor and her jacket on a chair and that, together with some wall cupboards over the bed and a tiny wardrobe, comprised the furniture in the tiny room. A minute washbasin in the alcove created by the wardrobe, a bed-head light and a window looking to the side, in the wall against which was the bed and another, looking to the rear, beside the wash-basin, completed the amenities. To the left of her door was the lavatory door; to the right, the door to the shower cubicle. A kitchen with a sink and Calor gas stove, narrow like a ship's galley, led into the living-room beyond which was another sleeping cabin like hers. That made up the mobile home which she was to share with another girl, as yet unmet.

She was weary, worn and totally relieved that she had walked into another job as easily and as much by chance as the last one. This, however, was a very different kettle of fish - a fairly large riding school. Two mobile homes housed the grooms on the yard and a big house the proprietor and his wife, two instructors and six resident pupils.

Sam did not want to think of the journey that had brought her here. She had walked and taken 'bus rides for four days, twice sleeping rough, twice in farm B.& B. places and on the fifth day she had seen the signboard saying Croft Equestrian Centre, Props: Major & Mrs. Moxon. She had walked in and found Mrs. Moxon, a tall, blonde woman of middle-age who had looked her over sharply, admitted to being short-handed for the Summer and agreed to try her.

"A week's trial, either side. Shall probably only want you for three months though. It's quieter through the winter."

Sam had nodded, only too glad to put an end to her travels, during which she had suffered every possible reaction to her departure from the safety of the Randall's home and company. Several times she had thought of turning back but she knew they did not need her and the knowledge that she had an eventual goal near Ringwood drew her on eastwards. But the idea of joining her relatives there and the inevitable explanations that must follow, held her back. The full tragedy of what had happened to her a year ago flooded over her again. The memory of her baby's feeble cry made her want to weep. She was achingly homesick but she knew she could not go back to face her father, yet. So she pressed on, not knowing, nor caring greatly, where she was going nor what she was going to do. So, now she was here, a haven of work, at least.

The work was very different to the casual, friendly atmosphere at the Randalls' There were twelve horses on the clients' yard and the grooms each took responsibility for three plus whatever children's ponies were needed in from the paddocks. There was a smaller yard with some well-schooled horses used by the instructors or star pupils and looked after by working pupils or paying students.

The students wore fawn breeches and black boots with pale blue shirts and navy blue ties with a navy sweater if the weather were cold. The grooms also wore the shirts, ties and sweaters with blue jeans and either wellingtons or short boots according to the job they were doing. The garments were obtainable from the tack shop on the premises and Sam forked out from her savings for them. She had not spent much while she was at Fallowfield and was to get a much bigger salary at the Croft. The jodhpurs and boots she had, she was glad to find, were suitable for when they had to exercise horses that were not wanted for lessons.

Stable routine was good, standards high and she found her riding compared very favourably with the other three grooms and most of the students. Both the Major and Mrs. Moxon gave instruction, one of the other instructors was their son and the other a rather pretty and cheerful young woman. The grooms were expected to attend certain lectures, had some riding instruction and were encouraged to aim for qualifications. The fact that Sam had five '0' levels was to her credit and she agreed to try for the Assistant Instructors' Certificate.

Stable management and horsemastership lessons were taken by the son, James Moxon, in a large room at the back of the house. Riding lessons for the grooms and working pupils were taken by the woman instructor, Vivi Deane.

Sam enjoyed them all. She had not had consistent instruction before and Vivi was cheerful and encouraging. The theory classes were like being back at school except that the teacher wore breeches and boots usually, if he had just come off the yard, was young and good looking and aware of the attraction that his standing and garb had for the mainly female pupils.

Sam's caravan partner was a rather well-developed girl called Liz. She looked at Sam's thin figure, in T-shirt and jeans, somewhat enviously as she struggled into her non-bounce bra.

"How do you manage to keep so slim?" she asked. "You eat as much as I do!"

"Just naturally skinny" said Sam. "Come on - we mustn't keep our Jimmy waiting."

Liz pulled on a shirt and they left the caravan to walk up to the house for the afternoon's stable management lecture. Although it was late afternoon, the August day was still hot and rather muggy. At first the house struck a little cool after the sunshine outside but as they sat at the tables in the lecture room they could feel the stuffy heat and the sweat breaking on their skin. There were six of them in the class. At least three of them, though Sam, cynically, had a crush on James.

He came in on the dot of five o'clock, looking cool in a fresh white shirt, tie and cotton breeches.

"Now, don't forget we have a lecture/demonstration at the beginning of next month" he said, taking up his stance by the blackboard. "Dressage. By Ben Thorn, the international rider."

As if we didn't know, thought Sam, doodling on the note-pad.

"We shall want guinea-pigs for him" went on James. "Liz can do the preliminary level, Sam, you do the novice and Vivi and I will do the others. That ought to be a reasonable cross-section for Mr. Benjamin Thorn."

"Benedict" said Sam.

"What?"

"His name is Benedict" said Sam.

James stared at her, a bit disconcerted.

"Oh - yes - I believe it is. He's usually known as Ben. Have you met him?"

"His Aunt runs the school in the next village to mine, in Devon. I worked there for a bit."

"Oh. Did he instruct you at all?"

"Yeah. And his father, Dan Thorn."

"The - Spanish Riding School man?"

Sam nodded. James continued to regard her, fascinated, for a while. Then he called for their attention and began the lesson.

The little exchange must have rankled - or the stuffy heat was trying to the temper. They had entered into a discussion on matching pupils to horses and the weight a horse could be expected to carry relative to size and build.

"You can hardly weigh anything, Sam" remarked James. "Are you sure you're not a little boy? You've got tiny boobs:"

"Yeah" said Sam, flicking a glance at him. "Like your willy, I expect."

A moment's silence was followed by a burst of laughter which relieved the atmosphere and in which James had the grace to join.

"Sorry, Sam" he said. "I agree - personal remarks are out of order."

"How could you say that to James?" asked Liz as they walked back to the caravan.

"Why not? Why should men make comments on your figure - and you can't?" retorted Sam. "If somebody said you had a big bum, would you like it?"

"No." Liz giggled. "But I could hardly make a similar remark in return!"

Back in the caravan they started to prepare their supper.

"What did he mean about Ben Thorn's father being the Spanish Riding School man?" asked Liz.

"He helped to rescue some of the horses at the end of the war" said Sam. "And learned to ride them and school them." She thought of the tall, slight figure of the now elderly Squire Thorn and the crisp banknote he had given her which she still kept tucked away for use 'as a last resort - to bring you home'. The memory of the kindness and the comfort it had given her made her feel homesick for the May days at Thornwood and she looked into Liz's lively, expectant eyes and smiled. "He's a nice man. Gypsy-ish. Lean and brown. Quite old, now, of course."

"Why did you leave there?"

"I had to get away from home. Had a row with my Da." Sam took plates out of the little oven and dished up their supper. "Come on, let's eat."

They were hacking out a few days later, Liz, Sam and James, cooling off the horses after a schooling session. Liz was one of the three in the stable management class who vied for James's favour - the remaining two in the class were boys and Sam did not think that they - nor James - had any leanings in that direction. So she rode along happily, relaxing her horse and letting Liz and James ride on a little ahead, talking and laughing together. What happened she did not see. Something must have startled James's mare - or bitten her - and she threw a great buck which sent him flying, landing half in a bed of nettles at the side of the lane. Fortunately the mare then stood still and Sam jumped off her horse and thrust its reins and the mare's reins into Liz's hands.

James was getting up, cursing under his breath and holding his arm. For a moment Sam wondered if he had broken it but she saw, below the rolled-up sleeve, the reddening and swelling of nettle stings all up his forearm and on the side of his face. She chuckled and cast around, snatching up half-a-dozen big dock leaves and bruising them in her hands.

"Here" she said. "Let me wrap these round your arm."

She plastered them deftly and pulled down his shirt sleeve, fastening it to secure them. Then she pulled another dockleaf and held it out.

"Hold that to your cheek" she said.

"Whew: That feels better" he acknowledged. "Lucky there were docks here."

"Where there's nettles, there's docks" she retorted and took her horse's reins from Liz. "You ought to be all right by the time we get back."

"Thanks, Sam. No - hard feelings, then?"

"None" she said and left it at that.

"Do you like James?" asked Liz, a little wistfully, when they were changing in the caravan. "He seems to be taking notice of you." She compared Sam's willowy figure with her own buxom form.

"You can have him" said Sam. "I'm not interested." She paused and flicked a grin at Liz. "It's all right! I'm not interested in girls, either!"

Liz laughed.

"Good! But you are very boyish, ar'n't you?

Sam pulled a comb through her short curls.

"I got two brothers" she said. "I expect Ma used the same pattern." But she thought of Nat and Josh and knew they were of Reuben's build and she was of a different style.

Chapter 8

Sam eased her shoulders under her pale blue shirt: she could feel the sweat-damp from the mugginess of the evening - or from her nervousness as she sat on her horse, waiting to ride into the school where Ben Thorn was just ending the novice session. Once James had learned that she had been taught by Ben, he had changed her place in the line. Liz had done the preliminary test, one of the boys had been put in the novice phase, Sam to the elementary and Vivi to do the medium level. James himself had opted out and was sitting with the students, ready to explain or clarify what Ben said, if necessary. Ben's wife, Beth was there, too, a slight, intense girl, some years younger than Ben, an excellent rider and in line to inherit an aunt's estate, in the next village to Lydston. Sam felt pleased that they were all from Devon and experienced a twinge of longing for the spreading Moor. Another year, she promised herself - it should be all right to face her father again, then - and she would see her two-year-old 'brotherson'. She wondered what they had called him. She never asked when she wrote to her Grandmother to send the £10 note and the old woman was not a letter-writer. Becca had not written at all, nor the boys - nor had Crispin. She wondered if he had thought to enquire at all about where she was or what she was doing. But she did not feel let down nor deserted. They were there - they would be there- when she went back. Until that time, she was content. The door to the school opened and Bill came out on the novice horse. He grinned at her and signed to her to go in. She smoothed down her tie, checked that the tie-pin securing it was straight - as she knew it was - and rode in.

Ben greeted her, smiling.

"Like old times, Sam" he said. "Let me try the horse and see what he can do."

She watched him with his easy seat and tender hands, walking the horse round, trotting, a short, quiet canter and then mounted again and gave herself totally to following his instructions, to making the horse carry out his requests, controlled, cadenced, fluent, all the time conscious of the impulsion necessary to perform the required movements. She was glad that she was riding old Floristan, a well-schooled, obedient yet spirited gelding, with whom she got on well.

When Ben had demonstrated what points he wanted to make to the students, he turned to her.

"Do you still remember Test 22?" he asked. "I know you've done it. Right. Go ahead." Sam went through the test, remembering the last time she had ridden it under Dan Thorn's direction, almost hearing him taking her through the movements. When she had finished and halted to salute, there was silence.

"Sam - that was almost my father doing that" accused Ben. He turned to the audience.

"I think you have seen an Elementary Test ridden just about as well as it could be. What a splendid old horse! Thank you, Sam."

She turned Floristan and rode out of the school, signing to Vivi, who was waiting to go in.

She was pleased with her performance and sprawled on

the caravan banquette after their supper that evening, thinking it over. Liz was browsing through a magazine at the table, reading out little snippets which Sam heard vaguely through her thoughts. She had managed to have a short talk with both Ben and Beth but they said they had not been home recently and had no news of her family. She accepted this without question, not noticing Beth's slight hesitation before replying.

"It says here" remarked Liz, again. "That cows are responsible for a lot of the pollution because they give off methane gas when they fart."

Sam pulled herself together and chuckled.

"Imagine what happens when they drive herds of cattle across the prairies" she said. "Particularly if the cowboys eat as many baked beans as they say."

Liz giggled.

"I hadn't thought of that" she said.

Liz was a pleasant companion. She had a placid nature and treated the horses with a gentle firmness, like a well-trained nanny. Her riding was good, her relaxed attitude seeming to calm the most nervous animal. She and Sam were the most likely ones on the junior staff to get their A.I. certificate and Sam hoped that she would not hear from Mrs. Moxon that she would only be required for the three months mentioned when she joined them.

As October came and passed and winter began to make the early mornings a penance rather than a joy to be up and about, Sam felt safe. She would be seventeen and a half years old in January, the age at which she could take the examination and she reckoned the quiet winter evenings were ideal for sitting down to study.

During the day there were more horses to exercise as daily pupil numbers dropped and there were fewer resident students. James Moxon and Vivi Deane did most of the instructing and schooled some of the more advanced horses so, apart from their lessons, Liz and Sam did most of the riding out.

At Christmas, all the pupils and most of the staff departed. Major and Mrs. Moxon with James and Vivi Deane remained, together with Liz, whose parents had split up and Sam. Minimal exercising was done; the horses were fed, watered, groomed and turned out in the fields in New Zealand rugs for three or four hours in the middle of the day.

Liz and Sam were invited into the house for Christmas lunch - in effect, dinner - and, after the horses had been settled in their stables again, were despatched to their caravan with gaily-wrapped gifts and a chunk of Christmas cake. On the evening of Boxing Day, there was a drinks party to which local friends and clients were invited and Sam got out her bright skirt and the gypsy blouse, gathered and embroidered, which her Gran had packed in the hold-all. She had kept her hair fairly short ever since it had been cropped in her fever and it clustered in black curls over her head. Liz, coming from the bedroom at her end, gaped in envious admiration.

"That's smashing" she said and turned her back to Sam. "Do me up."

She had on a quite attractive silk frock that did its best for her figure. Sam had gathered that she was not kept short of pocket money from her parents and she seemed to spend it wisely. They pulled on anoraks over their finery against the cold of the evening and walked across to the house.

After that, they fell back into the routine of work and study except for those who decided to stay up to see in the New Year. The rest of the staff came back and the new intake of resident pupils. Liz and Sam settled into peaceful evenings with their books.

It was a fairly mild winter which was as well for them and the other two grooms for the caravans could be draughty. Sam found it unseasonal and was disturbed in her concentration one evening when thunder growled in the distance and she had to close the curtains against the flashes of lightning. To Sam, thunderstorms belonged to the summer. They came out of a spell of heavy heat with a sudden wind to herald them and a downpour of cooling rain upon the grateful earth and left behind clear air and soft, blue skies. But a thunderstorm in winter was unnatural. She listened to it resentfully and fretted that the rain delayed. Liz soothed her and was delighted to hear the first heavy drops on the caravan roof and see Sam relax.

She often wondered about Sam. She knew she had left home because she had fallen out with her father and that their backgrounds were very different. She didn't ask to know any more. They got on well. They liked each other and were able to live in close proximity without rubbing each other up the wrong way.

So, in their little enclosure, at the table where they ate their meals or studied for their exams, read books, wrote letters or watched the small TV., they existed in harmony together, learning a little more about each other but never reaching any great intimacy.

One evening, Liz, sighing, closed her Manual of Horsemanship and said "Are you really not interested in men?"

Sam looked up.

"Not really."

"Really not - or not really not?"

Sam chuckled.

"I was brought up with two brothers. It's never struck me that boys were something to get excited about. I suppose I might - meet an exciting one - one day."

"I haven't any brothers:". said Liz "Or sisters."

Sam nodded. She had known Liz for an only child, indulged by each of her separated parents and getting no pleasure from either of them. She found consolation indulging herself but was generous in sharing the chocolates or cakes she bought. Sam was fortunate in not suffering from a sweet tooth and could accept sparingly or reject. Liz would sigh, remark on their figures and select another chocolate.

A little flurry of snow after a couple of cold days at the end of January marked their winter and then returned to soft, damp days in February. In the third week of that month came their examinations.

Six of them were taking it: Three from the Croft Equestrian Centre and three from outside. At 8.15 they assembled with Major and Mrs. Moxon and met the three examiners, were told what the agenda would be and were then handed over to an invigilator in the lecture room where the papers with questions on Minor Ailments were laid out ready for them. The three Croft girls wore their breeches and boots, pale blue shirts and navy ties and pullovers. Two of the other girls wore breeches, boots, shirts and hacking jackets and the third was wearing a stock and show jacket and looked a bit miserable about it. They all had hunt caps and gloves which they put down on a side table.

Sam, because she was interested in the treatment of ailments - both by standard veterinary medicine and by her Gran's remedies - was able to write freely on each question but she noticed Liz floundering and she knew it was because Liz had tried to memorize what the book said without really understanding why and it came to her later, thinking it all over, that the reason why she had not done very well in maths was because, although she could memorize the formulae she hadn't really grasped the principles behind them. She just hadn't got that sort of mind she decided and poor Liz had not got the sort of mind that would assimilate the principles behind the treatment of ailments or the basics of nutrition.

Their little group was then divided between the examiners to do stable management, horsemastership and teaching in the school and so to a break for lunch after which came equitation and jumping. Sam felt really lucky when she drew Floristan as her mount for equitation and a rather fiery, eager but controllable jumper.

At the end of the day she felt tired but moderately confident and they all went to the students' dining-room with the Moxons and the three examiners for tea. Then the Chief Examiner told them their results and they were able to discuss with the examiners how they had done in each section and where they had gone wrong or where they might have done better.

Sam had passed. She was particularly commended on her written paper and her riding. Liz had failed with her paper and her teaching. The other Croft student had passed and one of the outside students - the one in the show jacket who had been riding and showing ponies since she was six years old. Sam felt that, taken all round, the examiners had made a fair judgement though she was sorry for the failed ores who would have the expense a second time. Though, with Liz, she thought, that would not be a problem.

In actual fact, she found that in one way Liz was better off than she. The other Croft student was going back to a job at her parents' riding school. The Moxons were prepared to keep Liz on until she had her next attempt in three months' time; but they had no vacancy for a newly-qualified Assistant Instructor. So Sam faced the prospect of setting forth on her journeyings again.

They were prepared to keep her in her present situation while she applied for other jobs but Sam decided, as March came in fair, that she would take her chance on the open road, so to speak, as she had before. She thought about

Joan Calmady-Hamlyn

returning home and wondered if they would take pride in her achievement. But she saw her father's angry, horrified face, her brothers aghast, her mother's agonised compassion and she knew she could not go back to face them yet. The child would be close on a year old now.

So she sat down to write her weekly letter to her Gran and told her of her success and enclosed an old, non-crinkly ten-pound note to help keep her 'brotherson'.

Chapter 9

Sam was not sure which direction to take this time. The thought of her mother's family in the New Forest had kept her heading eastwards up to now. But she was beginning to convince herself that she did not want to join up with her relations and she thought she might head north and make a start on the curve that would face her west and homeward again.

Also, she had collected a certain amount of extra luggage and she would no longer be able to proceed far on foot. She stood, on the morning of her departure from Croft, beside her bed, methodically folding garments and stowing them away in her canvas holdall. Liz, still eating her breakfast toast, leaned against the door-jamb, sorrow-fully.

"I shall miss you" she said.

"Yeah. I'll miss you - all of you. Take care of old Floristan."

Mrs. Moxon had given her pay the evening before and with the Major had wished her goodbye and good luck; she had made her farewells to James and Vivi and thought that, if she ever came back that way, she would find them married; and to her other colleagues so all that remained was a quick hug with Liz and she was on her way.

She wondered if she should retrace her steps and stop off

at Fallowfield on the way back home. Lissa would have had the baby now and might be glad of extra help. But things were never the same, second time around and though at times like this, really depressing moments, she was almost sick with longing for the moor, she knew she was not ready to go back, yet. So she struggled to gain a mood of optimism and set forth.

The early Spring weather helped. It was a fresh, sunlit morning and promised to warm up through the day. She had the long boots she had acquired strapped to the holdall and had also bought an ex-Army haversack which took her hat and short boots and bumped rather clumsily against her hip. She took a 'bus from the village to the nearest town and then found somewhere to stay and dumped her luggage.

She spent a couple of nights there, had her hair cut, went to a cinema matinee and made good use of the library reading room where she studied such local and neighbouring newspapers as they had there.

There was only one advertisement that interested her: 'Groom wanted for three children's ponies and lady's hack. Qualified/experienced. Live in. Tel: Radleigh 34907. She asked the librarian where Radleigh was and was told 'on the edge of the moor'.

She lay awake that night, pondering. On the moor - Exmoor, of course, not her own moor. Would it be for a sole groom or would there be another who looked after hunters - stag-hunters, she thought, being Exmoor.

Children's ponies in a private household would be something new. She had not done too badly for new experiences and new accomplishments so far - a rather sketchy establishment at Fallowfield - but she had got her driving licence there. A very efficient business at Croft - and she had got her Assistant Instructor's certificate there. So what could she acquire from - and what would she give to - three ponies and a lady's hack?

She took another 'bus next day and, after a couple of hours, got off at a crossroads where a finger-post pointed to Radleigh, lm.

The day was a bit dull and had been misty. She had on an anorak over her shirt and jeans and boots and her cropped dark curls were bare. She humped her haversack over her shoulder, picked up her holdall and started walking.

She could see below her a small village, Radleigh, she reckoned. On her left, as she walked along, tall, ornate iron gates and on the stone posts Radleigh and a small notice Radleigh Stud, lst. left. Hardly the home of three ponies and a hack, she thought but might be worth a try if the advertized vacancy had been filled.

The first turning left proved to be a gravelled lane marked 'Private Road to Radleigh Stud' and Sam paused to consider. Was it worthwhile going up there and inquiring or should she keep to her plan of telephoning from the village and getting directions?

She put down her holdall and unslung her haversack and looked again towards the moor. The village was out of sight but must be quite near.

A mild commotion, a child's shriek and the sound of a galloping pony turned her head sharply to look up the lane again. A grey pony, the rope of the headcollar trailing and threatening to trip it up, was tearing towards her. Behind, she could see a child running and other figures behind again.

Sam whistled softly and lifted her arms. The flattened ears came forward, pricked interestedly, the wild eyes focussed on her and the pony slowed and trotted up to her, coming to a halt and letting her pick up the rope. She stood, waiting for the boy running down the lane.

He was, she thought, about ten and his face was distressed and blotchy.

"Oh, thanks - thank you!" he jerked out. "Something startled him and he pulled the rope out of my hand." He took it from her and turned to face the three following him - a girl of about fourteen, a younger boy of seven or eight and, walking behind, obviously their father, a man in cavalry cords and a cashmere sweater.

"He caught him - he stopped him" said the first boy.

"You are a fool, letting go like that" said the girl.

The man came up, smiling.

"Have you thanked him?" he asked his son and looked at Sam. "Thank you. It was brave of you to stand your ground. He was travelling quite fast."

"That's O.K." said Sam. She thought she had probably reached her goal.

"All right, Mark" said the man. "Take Cloudy and get him into the paddock, this time. Go on, Sue - you and Harry go, too."

He watched them go up the lane with the now quiet pony and turned back to Sam. He had seen her bags on the ground.

"Now, then, lad, where are you going? Perhaps I can help you on your way?"

"I was going to Radleigh to ask about a groom's job - for three ponies and a hack" said Sam, with her eyes on the three children.

The man started to laugh.

"And you reckon you've found it?" he said. "Well - you're right. I did advertize. But I must confess I had someone a bit older in mind. What are you - sixteen?"

"I'm nearly eighteen" said Sam, seriously. "I've got a driving licence and I'm a BHSAI - since the end of February."

He twinkled, responsively.

"That's impressive" he agreed. "What's your name?"

"Sam Lee."

He looked at her cropped dark curls and brown face.

"Romany?"

"My grandparents were travelling gypsies" said Sam. "But Gran has a cottage in Devon and my parents have a small-holding and keep ponies and cattle."

"Devon? What are you doing on Exmoor?"

"I was at the Croft Equestrian Centre for some months to take the A.I. exam. and then just thought I'd look around for work in the area. I've got two older brothers at home so I'm not needed there."

He nodded.

"I'm Peter Churston" he said. "You saw my three children and one of the ponies you'll look after. You're probably light enough to exercise that one when necessary and Harry's pony will lead off any of the others. My daughter has a fourteen-two Connemara and my wife's hack is fifteen-two and well-mannered. That and the Connemara are stabled at night at present and the two smaller ponies are out in the paddock. Think you could manage? The kids are all at day schools."

"Yes, sir" said Sam. "Reckon I could manage."

"Very well. We'll give it a trial. You can have a room in the house if you like or there's a one-berth caravan if you can look after yourself."

Sam, considering her ambiguous sex, decided on the caravan. It would mean additional pay if she looked after herself and greater freedom.

"Come on, then" said Churston. "We'll take your bags up and you can look round."

They walked up the lane, noting that two ponies were safely in one of the paddocks and the children were out of sight.

At the top of the lane were what were obviously the Stud

buildings but Churston turned off to the left and they came to a stable-yard beyond which was a large house. The yard had a stone block of boxes and tack-room and hay-store and a stretch of grass beyond which was a covered school. On the far side of the yard was a blue-painted mobile home, its wheels skirted and concealed and a couple of stone steps leading up to the door. A trough at their foot contained earth and some primulas. It looked very settled.

"Here you are" said Peter Churston. "Go and see if you think you can make out here and when you are ready come up to the house. We'll have some tea and sort out what supplies you'll need to get." He dumped Sam's haversack that he had been carrying, inside the door and walked off.

"Considerate" thought Sam and nipped into the loo.

The caravan was well equipped, she found. Beside the loo was a shower compartment. In the kitchen, a Calor gas stove stood beside the sink which had a good-sized water heater over it. Under the work-top was tucked a refrigerator/freezer and a portable sink-top washing-machine which would, thought Sam, take underwear or a shirt and pair of breeches. In the sitting/dining area she found a small wood-burner and a portable television set. The bedroom was beyond the shower and loo with a good-looking bed, a narrow wardrobe and chest of drawers and a wash-hand basin. Sam reckoned she could make out here very well.

She put her bags down in the bedroom, washed her hands, ran fingers through her tight curls and went back to the kitchen, off which the door gave. On the work-top were a couple of keys on a key-ring and she slipped them into her pocket, dropped the catch on the Yale lock and went out.

The house was long, two-storey and built of honey-coloured stone with weathered russet tiles. The door facing the yard was obviously a back or side door, the main frontage being towards the drive from the road. Sam tried the back-door and found herself in a passage off which the kitchen opened. The whole family appeared to be gathered by the Aga on which the kettle was coming to the boil.

"Come in, Sam" said Churston. "My wife will sort out your shopping list with you, after tea."

Charlotte Churston smiled at Sam, noting her youth and her slight figure, thankful that she - or he, as they thought - was young and not another despot like the old groom who had just retired.

"You're a bit different to old Perkins, who has just gone" she said. "But I'm sure we shall get on very well."

"Yes, Ma'am" said Sam. "You just let me know how you like things to be done." She sensed rather than saw Charlotte's relief and realised there might be something to sort out there. An old family groom, a dominant old servitor, who would do things as he wanted, she guessed. She must tread, gently.

Chapter 10

Sam learned a great deal about her job from the children's chatter. As. she had suspected, Mrs. Churston had been intimidated by Perkins who had been groom to the children's grandfather and had taught their father to ride. Their mother had learned to ride in the modern school of dressage and eventing whereas Perkins only reccgnized one seat on a horse and that the old hunting seat. His scarce concealed scorn had frozen Charlotte out of the stables and he had used her horse, Radleigh Petrella, to escort the children on hacks. Peter Churston ran the farm and rode a horse from the Stud which was still supervised by his father, Sir George.

"But Mark and I don't need escorting now" said Susan. "We're quite able to go out, alone."

Sam, seeing the anxiety in Mark's eyes, thought not.

"You should take your Mother out" she said. "And I'll take Mark and Harry out when either your Shadow or Petrella need exercising. Or you could all go out with your Mother. You could help her look after Mark and Harry, Susan, couldn't you? I'm sure she'd enjoy it."

"Mummy doesn't ride much, now" said Mark's worried little voice.

"I don't think that's because she doesn't want to" said

Sam, hanging up the bridle she had been cleaning. "There!
That's the tack. You'd better go in for your lunch."

She was rewarded when Charlotte came to the stables
on Sunday morning and said that Susan had suggested she
ride out with them.

"You're all right, Sam, are you?" she asked. "No reasons
for you not going out?"

"No, Ma'am" said Sam. "The children thought you'd like
to take them out and it does seem a pity you don't get out
on Petrella more often."

Charlotte considered her for a moment.

"Yes - all right" she said. "We'll go out at ten o'clock. And
you will come out with me tomorrow morning after I have
taken them to school."

Sam, satisfied, decided to muck out the boxes
thoroughly while the horses were out: it would give her a
chance to wipe down the walls, too.

She was disturbed during her morning, when, with her
shirt sleeves rolled and jeans and wellies on, she was
swabbing the stable walls with a large sponge and a bucket
of hot, soapy water.

"Bit young for this, lad" said a voice behind her.

Sam turned: at the stable door, a lean little jockey-like
figure in trousers and riding jacket with a flat cap on a
grizzled head. She had no doubt who it was.

"Old enough, Mr. Perkins" she said.

He came further in and gazed around at the loose boxes.
She had the doors open, ready for the riders' return and the
straw banked high.

"The Missus out with the kids?" he said. "She'll be turning
out every day, if you let her. She will."

"Why not?" said Sam. "They're her horses."

"They're not her horses. She don't own them, she don't.
They're his."

"Whether they'm his or hers, 'tis the same thing" retorted

Sam, pitching her Devon accent against his Somerset.
"Anyway, Mr. Perkins, perhaps you'll be good enough to let
me get on with my work. And, if you want to visit my
stables again, get Mr. Churston's permission." She turned
back to her bucket and picked up the soapy sponge.

Churston looked in a little later.

"I gather you've had a passage of arms with Perkins" he
remarked.

"Yeah. Maybe I shouldn't have - ?"

"I don't think you'd accept much advice from him.
Anyway - he says he reckons you've taken over and he
won't be visiting you again! My father knows all the old
customs, so don't worry."

"Maybe I was over sharp - "

"Don't worry! My wife was always terrified of him. She'll
enjoy her riding again, now." He nodded to Sam and went
out.

She drew a breath of relief and started clearing up.
When the hack and the three ponies returned, everything
was neat and spotless. She took Petrella and Shadow into
the stables and Mrs. Churston and Susan untacked them
while she went to help the two boys with the ponies,
Cloudy and Rumpus.

The following weekend, Charlotte Churston was away
and Sam prepared to ride out on Petrella with the children,
home from school. They were expected to tack up the own
ponies though Sam had groomed them ready.

"Mark doesn't want to ride today" said Sue, coming into
the stables. "His face hurts. Gran'dad reckons he's got
blocked sinuses or something."

Sam looked at the boy. He was heavy-eyed and had a
blotchy flush on his face.

"I will ride if you think I should" he said.

"No. I'll lead Cloudy from Petrella" said Sam. "You can
go and lie down in the caravan if you want." She watched

him trail across the grass and looked at Sue. "Does your Mother know he's like this?"

"He was all right when she left. She won't be back till tonight. But I'll tell Dad at lunchtime when he comes in."

Sam nodded and put a bridle on the pony. She watched Sue and Harry mount then let Sue hold Cloudy until she had mounted Petrella.

They went up to the edge of the moor, through Radleigh village and kept to a steady trot because of the led pony. They were on the moorland track when another horse approached: Sir George riding one of the youngsters from the Stud.

Sam had met him once or twice. He was a man in the early sixties, she imagined with a lean, horseman's body and a taut, weather-browned face. The children greeted him happily and he waved them on and aligned his horse beside Sam. She said "Good morning, sir" politely and he indicated the pony.

"Mark not out?"

"No. He didn't seem too good."

"He doesn't seem to have been too well since Christmas. I must get him to see the doctor. And how are you, young Sam? Settled in?"

"Yes, sir, thank you."

"I hear good reports of you. Been over to the Stud, yet?"

"No, sir."

"Good. I suggest you don't - unless my son brings you over to see it. A good-looking young lad like you might be subjected to some - horse-play."

"Yes, sir."

He glanced at her, sharply.

"You know what I am saying?"

"Yes, sir. You got some queers over there?"

"I'm glad you don't call them gays. A most unsuitable

description. No, I hope not. But you might get thrown in the trough."

Ahead of them, Sam glimpsed two more riders. Although quite distant, she could see who they were and glanced at Sir George to see if he had caught sight of them. From the set of his head and his narrowed eyes, he had: his son and the Master's wife.

"I think the ponies should go back, now" she said and called to Sue. She, however, was not so diplomatic, as she and Harry rode up.

"That's Daddy and Mrs. Bilston" she said, indignantly. "If he'd said he was riding on the moor we could have gone with him."

"I expect he's been a lot further than Rumpus could go" said Sam. She thought if he'd been over to the Hunt kennels, a great deal further.

"Is Mark going to be fit for school, tomorrow, Susan?" asked Sir George.

"I don't know, Gran'dad. Sometimes - it doesn't last long."

"Is he like this often? I must get your mother to have him checked up." He waved the children on ahead. "I've often wondered what I would do if I had a crippled child. One hears awful tales" he remarked. "Well, young Sam, what do you think?"

"Depends on what you think about the soul" said Sam. "If you believe that souls move on into a new body when the old one's dead, then you'd let a crippled baby die."

"Could a mother do that?"

Sam shrugged.

"I wouldn't know. I just think it would be awful to have to go through life with a severe disability. But they say - they're happy - usually."

"Perhaps it's good for the soul - to have one disabled reincarnation?"

"Maybe." Sam chuckled. "Trouble is - we don't know, do we, what we've been?"

Sir George laughed.

"You're a strange lad, young Sam" he said. "Where'd you get these ideas?"

"I don't know. Used to do a lot of reading when I was at school. And Gran'ma used to talk to me a lot."

"Your relapsed gypsy grandmother?"

"Yeah. She gave up travelling when Gran'pa died and came to live near Ma - Da wasn't a gypsy - he was horse-trading."

"On the edge of Dartmoor. How does our moor compare with yours?"

Sam grinned.

"I like mine better."

They were coming into the village now and up the hill to Radleigh House where they turned up the lane to the Stud and Sir George rode straight on while Sam and the two children turned off to the stable-yard.

"Gran'dad likes you" said Sue. "He talks to you a lot."

"He's easy to talk to" said Sam, handing over Cloudy's bridle and dismounting.

A rather wan Mark came down from the caravan and helped to put the ponies out in the field with their mid-day feed. Sam watched the three children go off to the house and wondered about her conversation with their Grandfather.

Chapter 11

Sam had got the family fairly well sorted out by now: Sir George, almost an old-fashioned dandy with his long-skirted hacking jackets and well-creased fawn trousers. She had a faint suspicion that he could be of that fraternity whose unsuitable nickname gave him such horror. With his weathered face, smooth grey hair and crisp voice, he could be or he could be a 'man for the ladies' or even, she decided, faithful to the memory of his five years' dead wife. Peter Churston was definitely one for the ladies and was, Sam reckoned, causing his wife a good deal of heartache. Susan probably recognized this although she assumed a general air of casual cheerfulness. Of the two boys, Harry, she felt, was the natural heir to the establishment, a robust, no-nonsense lad while poor fragile Mark would wilt under the burden of the title, the house, the Estate, the farm and the Stud.

The household, otherwise, was fairly orthodox - a live-in cook-housekeeper and two daily women from the village plus the 'old family retainer' though in this case not all that old but a woman in the late fifties who had been Charlotte's nursery governess and now, apart from keeping a general eye on the children, acted as part-time secretary-cum-telephone answerer - a useful general factotum.

They had ridden through the farm-yard and passed the farm workers' two cottages on several occasions but Sam had not, as yet, visited the stud. Remembering what Sir George had said, she was a bit doubtful when Susan, on hearing this, suggested that they go there together. It was the covering season now and they would be busy, Sue said but that should not prevent the two of them just going to have a look at the stallions and the visiting mares.

The place was well laid out and well kept. The four stallions had big looseboxes looking out on to a yard, with separate paddocks to run out in behind. The covering yard lay between them and the yard where the mares were kept. The foaling boxes were separate again and there were well-fenced paddocks where the mares and foals were turned out. The elderly stallionman was standing by the covering yard and Susan spoke to him, introducing Sam. The man looked her over.

"Yes - well - I should keep to your own neck of the woods, lad, if I were you. You look a bit too delicate for my lads here. And you, too, Miss Susan. You know your Dad doesn't like you here."

"Grandfather doesn't mind" she retorted but evidently didn't believe herself and excused her visit at once. "I only came to show Sam where it was."

They turned back the way they had come but two or three of the stud grooms were by the stallion boxes now.

"Hi, Sue - new boy friend?" came a call behind them.

"Shouldn't take him behind the stables" said another anonymous voice.

Sam glanced at Susan. The girl was scarlet but walked on in silence. Sam thought the last remark probably had some truth in it.

She found her days busy and fulfilling enough but the evenings lonely. She sadly lacked the company she had enjoyed at the Croft and had to make do with the small portable TV and the books she had found, in the caravan. It was too far to walk into and back from the village at night and she did not want to find herself with the stud staff at the local pub. She was beginning to think more and more of her beloved moor and decided that by the coming of Autumn she would be ready to make her way homeward.

The children were home for the Easter holidays now and Sam's mind wandered sometimes to a late March day last year. She heard her own screaming, accusing voice and the aghast faces of her family. Thereafter, she recalled little more until May Day Eve and her Grandmother's news. Only a vague recollection remained of the thin wail of the baby. Would he be getting like her brothers, her brotherson?

Susan, knocking on the caravan door and coming in, broke her reverie. The girl looked pale and shaken. Sam waved her to a banquette and waited.

"Mummy took Mark to the hospital" said Susan. "Doctor Hanson said he had to go for tests. They think he's got leukaemia."

"Poor Mark" said Sam, deliberately matter-of-fact. Susan looked taut and ready to break. "No wonder he always felt so tired."

"But he - he won't die, Sam, will he?"

Running footsteps, a thump on the door and a scarlet-faced Harry burst in.

"Sam - has Sue told you? He can't die - he can't! He's Daddy's heir - he'll be Sir Mark after Daddy. I'm not - I won't be Sir Harry!"

"If Mark dies, you will be" retorted Susan.

"But he - he's got to have all this - the house and - "

"Stop it:" roared Sam and the two heated children subsided, gazing at her with enormous eyes.

"What does it matter who's Sir This or Sir That and has the house? The main thing is Mark's health. The tests may be OK. In any case there are all sorts of treatments, now. So calm down. You've got to be a help to your brother and your parents."

The children exchanged a glance.

"Sorry, Sam" said Susan. "We just had to let go to someone."

"Yes, OK. You can always come and shout at me if it helps. But not at your Mum and Dad."

"We can always talk to you, Sam" said Harry. "You're not like the Stud boys. Perhaps it's 'cause you've got gypsy in you."

"Maybe" said Sam. "Maybe it's because I've got to know you better than the Stud boys-." She got up. "Like some tea?"

She made them tea in mugs with some chocolate biscuits and they sat side by side, their eyes withdrawn, brooding on this challenge that had entered their lives.

A brisk tap heralded Sir George at the door. His eyes went to the pair on the banquette and then to Sam. She turned on the electric kettle again, dunked a tea bag in a mug and gave it to him, putting the biscuit tin on the table. He helped himself, thoughtfully.

"Thanks, Sam" said Susan. "We'll come and ride tomorrow morning."

She and Harry went out and Sam watched them go, through the window, side by side, Harry's hand tucked in Susan's.

"They came to you for comfort, too?" said Sir George. "What is it about you, young Sam? Or is it Samantha?"

"Samaria" said Sam and put the children's mugs in the sink.

"Samaria? That's unusual. And why is Samaria masquerading as a boy?"

"Mark mistook me for one on the first day. It seemed easier to stay one."

"You don't mind whether you're boy or girl?"

"It doesn't matter. I'm neuter."

"My dear child! You're what?"

"I had a baby - about this time, last year. I was very ill and they took - everything away with the baby. Stop me being bad again, I expect."

"Being bad? Were you to blame for getting with child?"

"The woman always is, isn't she? Right from Adam. 'The woman tempted me, Lord and I did eat.' I was raped." She looked back at the scene on the sunlit river bank and the provocative, hateful red frock. The twinge of guilt was still there. She looked across at the man and his kind, concerned eyes made her cry out "It was my father - that's why I left home."

"And the child?"

"My mother took him. He'll be a year old - about now. I don't know the exact date. I was sick for over a month."

"Poor Sam" he said, gently. "You have suffered. That's why we come to you for comfort. Thank you for telling me. It will go no further. And I shall be so grateful if you can help the children through this time."

"I'll do my best" said Sam.

She went out, when Sir George had left, to check the ponies in the field and to do evening stables. Shadow and Petrella whickered at her entry and she took off their day rugs and brushed them over before putting on the thicker night rugs. They would soon be able to leave off day rugs, she thought and be out in the field for longer until, by May, they could be out all day and then, when the hot weather came, out all night and in stable for coolness during the day. It was a satisfying routine, she found and the horses seemed to do well on it though it was not an entirely natural life. But then, it wasn't natural for them to be saddled and bridled and ridden, hunted and jumped and so one had to compensate for that. She gave them their evening feed, filled the haynets ready to put up later on and went back to the caravan to get her supper.

Mark was waiting for her by the door.

Sam drew the child inside. She had left the heater on and the caravan was welcomely warm for, though March was going out like a lamb, the evenings were still chilly. She pulled off her boots and sat down beside Mark on the banquette. His eyes were withdrawn and she took him into her arms where he nestled, his head against her shoulder.

"I've wanted so long to feel well again" he said, sighing. "And now I know I never shall. I don't think it matters much now. It's just that I shall be so sad to leave here. I do love it so, the house and the gardens and the fields. You will look after Cloudy? I don't want to leave him but Harry will ride him well. I loved riding on the moor. And Sue - and Harry."

"Hush, now" said Sam, gently. "You have time, yet. You mustn't think about leaving them all, yet."

"No" he said, seriously. "I have time to enjoy them all - with the Spring coming. I shall see all my best places and - Sam - if we walked the ponies quietly, I could go up on the moor, again, couldn't I?"

"Yes, of course you could. Whenever you feel like it."

"I'm so glad you're here, Sam. Perkins wouldn't have understood. I must go back for supper. Mummy will wonder where I am." He smiled at her and got up. She stood at the door and watched him walk away in the twilight, waiting until his figure had diminished and was swallowed up by the house. Then she went within and began to prepare her meal.

Chapter 12

Sir George Churston sought out Sam again a week or so later. He came into the stables where she was mucking out Petrella's box and stood for a while watching her. She glanced at him, saw he was not ready to speak and went on, sorting wet and dry straw. He spoke, abruptly.

"The boy's not going to get better."

"No."

"The specialist offered treatment but did not think it would prolong his life appreciably." His voice was curt, almost resentful. Sam could recognize the frustrated hurt behind it. She paused and looked at him, leaning on her long-handled fork. "Charlotte wants to take him away - an extended holiday - show him something of the world. The poor child's seen nothing."

"Would he want that?" Sam thought of Mark's visit to her, his expression of love for his home, his pony, his brother and sister. "He might miss - his friends - all this."

"I don't want him to go" said Sir George, almost savagely. "He could die, miles from home... Oh, my God - why?"

"He has completed his mission." Sam was not sure where the words came from, whether from her Grandmother or some dimly-remembered reading.

"What?" The word shot from Sir George.

Sam struggled in. her mind to explain.

"It's - just - the idea that we have a purpose to fulfil on earth - and some people fulfil it earlier in life than others." She looked at his stricken face, apprehensively but he gave her a curt nod and went out. She thought he wept.

She noted that, since Mark's illness had been diagnosed, Peter Churston was more often at home and in company with Charlotte. They rode out together sometimes with the other two children who were now back at school. Mark still went occasionally, when he felt well enough. Sam had noticed Mrs. Bilston riding alone on the moor, not approaching Radleigh too closely but obviously on the look-out.

It did not surprise her when Charlotte and Peter came to the caravan one day when Susan and Harry were at school.

"My father says he told you that we were planning to take Mark to Europe for a month or so and you felt he might miss being here. Has he said anything to you?" said Peter.

"He only told me - once - how he loved being here and would miss Cloudy and Susan and Harry."

"But he's been here all his life" said Charlotte. "He must have the chance to see other places. The doctor says - he's got three to six months. We could take him, together." She glanced at Peter and Sam thought she wants him still. "It would be like a second honeymoon for us."

"You can't use his illness for that!" said Sam, horrified.

"Sam! Of course not! It's to show him London and Paris - Vienna - "

"Why?" said Sam, furiously. "He wants to be where he's happy and safe - and at peace with people he knows and loves and his pony and his 'special places'. He's not going to have time for memories."

Charlotte cried out and clutched Peter's arm. They both stared at Sam and she thought she had gone too far but knew she would not withdraw one word. She thought of the weary little boy being dragged round the sights of London and Paris, no doubt to the Spanish Riding School at Vienna, yearning for his home.

After what seemed an endless silence, Peter gave a queer little laugh.

"How right, Sam. It would be a wasted journey. You go and see these places so you can remember them when you're old..."

A tap on the-door heralded the appearance of Mark. He had on his jodhpurs and boots and looked straight at Sam, ignoring his parents.

"I want to take Cloudy to the moor" he said.

"We'll go and get him" said Sam and he put his hand in hers as they left the caravan.

Sam rode Shadow and they walked the ponies quietly through the village and up to the moor and the boy pointed out favourite places as they went.

"Mummy wants to take me to Europe" he said. "I think it's to get Daddy away from Mrs. Bilston. I don't want to go and Grandad doesn't want me to. I want to be here."

"I don't think she'll take you now" said Sam.

He flashed a look at her. He didn't remark on it but she knew he understood what they had been talking about in the caravan.

As she cleaned the tack that afternoon, Sam thought of the previous year, when April had been a lost month to her and she had only awakened on the last day when her Gran had told her that the morrow was May Day. Then she had spent three weeks getting into shape before starting off on her odyssey. She looked back over the year dispassionately. She felt no sorrow, no sense of loss; no emotion at all. Compassion for young Mark and his family, yes. A family with all they could wish for in life, yet lost, separated. Were they to be pulled together by this blow of fate?

She hung up Cloudy's bridle and put his saddle on the

wooden horse, her hand lingering on the smooth, polished seat. She thought she would not be cleaning tack for Mark, again.

May came in with beauty. A soft warmth leavened by gentle showers left over from the passed month. Leaves of every shade of green clothed the trees; golden daffodils Lent Lilies, had gone and silvery bluebells had taken their place.

In the middle of the month Susan and Harry were home for the half-term break. Sam groomed and tacked up Shadow and Rumpus for them and sent them out together to the moors. Then she took Petrella with Cloudy on a leading rein and exercised them both. When she got back, Mark was sitting on the caravan steps. She turned the hack and the pony out together quickly and went to him. He looked up at her and smiled.

"Sam, isn't it beautiful?" he said. "The sun is so warm and I can't see a cloud - the sky is all blue."

"It's perfect" she said. "I'm thirsty. Like some orange juice?"

"Yes, please." He followed her into the caravan and a little later she heard the other two ponies return.

When Susan and Harry had untacked and turned their ponies out to grass, they came to the caravan and found Sam and Mark sitting comfortably together on the banquette, with their glasses of orange.

"Help yourself" said Sam. "Orange juice or fizzy lemon."

"Fizzy for me" said Harry and Susan poured from the bottles. "It's great up on the moor. Just a little breeze so we had a canter but we didn't make them hot, Sam. They were quite cool when we got back, weren't they, Sue?"

"Yes. But it will be hot enough soon for them to be in stables by day, won't it, Sam?"

"By the end of the month, I expect" said Sam.

"I'm glad it's not too hot" said Mark, dreamily. "It all gets dried up and dusty but it's all fresh and green, now." He drew up his feet and curled against Sam. "I'm glad you had a good ride. You will look after Cloudy for me, Harry? I do love you and Sue."

Sam put an arm about him and glanced at Sue's stricken face.

"Harry" she said. "Run and fetch your Mother."

He put down his glass and looked into her eyes. Then he got up and slipped out of the door. Through the window she could see him running like a deer towards the house. Susan came and knelt in front of her.

"I'm so glad you're here, Sam" said Mark. His voice was very distant. "Tell them all I love them and how happy I was... and how beautiful it is..."

Sam looked down at his quiet face and gently closed the heavy eyelids. "He couldn't wait, Sue" she said. "He's gone."

Sue looked up at her, then down at her brother.

"He looks so - content" she whispered.

Running feet brought Peter Churston up the steps and into the caravan. He stopped, staring. Sue got up slowly and went to him.

"Sam" he said. "Gone? So quickly?"

"So happily" said Sam.

Harry burst in, followed by Charlotte, gasping and anxious.

"Peter - Sam - what is it?"

Harry plumped down on his knees where Sue had knelt. He put out a gentle hand and laid the back of it on his brother's face.

"He looks just - more asleep" he said, wonderingly.

Charlotte cried out.

"He is asleep! Oh, he is asleep, isn't he?"

Sam got up, the boy in her arms and put him into his father's arms.

"Yes" she said. "He said he loved you all and he was happy and it was very beautiful.'

They went out, a divided family, united in loss, the father carrying his son, the mother and daughter clasping each other and the wonder-struck little brother.

Sam gathered up the four glasses and put them into the sink and the bottles back into the refrigerator. Then she went out to check the ponies in the field and to clean the four sets of used tack.

She was not surprised to see Sir George that afternoon. He knocked on the caravan door just as she was brewing some tea and she gestured him in and put a mug of it into his hands. He took it and sat down.

Thank God they didn't go abroad" he said, abruptly.

"It was better this way" she agreed. "And he was so happy here."

"Yes. Sue said he was talking about the sun and the blue sky. Then how he loved them and Harry was to care for his pony. And then?"

"Then - he just went. He was ready and he went."

"You were with him, the three of you, you were with him till then. But then - is it a lonely step - into the dark?"

"Into the light" said Sam.

He put his fingers to his eyes, pressing down the lids, then released them with a sigh and took a gulp of tea.

"Into the light, young Sam" he repeated. "Yes, I will remember that."

Chapter 13

Sam stayed at Radleigh until the end of June; then she knew it was time for her to go. She had not attended Mark's funeral in the Church but took Cloudy on a leading rein and stood with him at the churchyard gate and Susan and Harry welcomed her with tremulous smiles as they came out and Harry buried his face in Cloudy's mane for a moment.

After she had told Peter Churston that she would leave in a month's time, Sir George came to the stables where she was cleaning tack.

"So you go on your journeyings again next month" he said.

"'Tis time" said Sam.

"Yes. Sue and Harry will be home for the Summer and can help Charlotte with the ponies. Would you like to take Cloudy?"

"No" said Sam. "Mark left him to Harry to care for. And Harry's getting too big for Rumpus now, who would suit your stallion man's little boy."

He gave a surprised laugh.

"You've got it all worked out, young Sam" he said. "Now - can I ask a favour of you?" Sam threw a questioning glance at him.

"The Hunt have a Midsummer ball in the village" he said. "Peter and Charlotte don't feel like attending. I must. So I thought I could use the other two tickets and take Susan now she's fifteen - and I hoped you would come and give us moral support. It would be Susan's first public dance."

Sam considered. A Hunt dance in the village would mean the ordinary followers, farmers, the Stud staff, more lowbrow than a hunt ball at the Manor. She visualised the grooms when she turned up in a skirt ... As she would be leaving soon after, it would not matter. She nodded.

"Yes, OK. Thank you. You want me to keep an eye on Susan?"

"And to enjoy yourself."

"Midsummer's Eve or Midsummer's Day?" she asked.

"Day - the 24th. I can't think why it's Midsummer's Day on the 24th. when Summer starts on the 21st."

"Summer starts on May Day" corrected Sam, softly.

"May Day?" he repeated, interested. "Fertility rites? 'Obby 'osses'? Of course! It was a holiday long before the Labour Government borrowed it from the Russians! I thought May was Springtime."

"Springtime - the beginning of growth - the awakening of the earth - starts in February" said Sam. "I think that's the trouble with the World. We've got out of step with the Seasons. And we muck around with the clocks and get out of step with the Sun and Moon. We're stupid."

"What a strange, wise child you are, Sam" Sir George said. "I must go."

Sam dressed in her gypsy skirt and the embroidered, gathered muslin blouse on the evening of the 24th. She put her silver buckled shoes on bare feet and twisted ribbons of green and red together to thread through her black curls, tying them in a knot behind her ear so that the ends fell over her shoulder. She was regarding the result, pensively in her looking-glass when Sir George and Susan came for her.

Charlotte had not dressed Susan - or Susan had not allowed her to - in young girl's white or pink simplicity. She wore a pale blue blouse with a neat, ruffled front and a shot-silk taffeta skirt of deep blue, soft enough to mould to her young figure but stiff enough to conceal its angular immaturity.

They both looked at Sam with startled appreciation.

"How pretty you look!" said Susan.

"When did you first realise Sam was a girl?" asked her Grandfather.

"I think - when I first saw her holding Mark. That was when I knew - though I had wondered before."

The village was quite large and quite full when the three of them entered, Sir George in Hunt evening dress and the two young girls on either side of him. For a moment there seemed to be a pause in the hum of conversation, then the Master, Major Bilston, came to greet them and asked Susan to dance and behind him was the Stud stallion man.

"Well - Miss Sam!" he said. "I believe my boy has you to thank for the use of Harry's pony. He's very chuffed. Will you dance this one with me?"

Sam thought over the evening as she packed her things, a week later. It had been a happy night and produced no difficult aftermath.

She had written to her Gran to tell her that she would get the early train to Exeter and take the 'bus from there to Moorcombe and finally the 'bus from there to Thornwood Church which was just along the lane from the cottage. As she had acquired so many more possessions she could not make the journey back as she had on her way out, though she had toyed with the idea of sending her bags and being free to walk or hitch-hike. But her canvas holdall and shoulder bag and boots could not really be sent on their own and she had the feeling, now that she had determined to go back, that she should go as quickly as possible and not loiter on the way.

She wondered what had gone on at home at Bellacombe and at Stony Gravel Cottage and if either of her brothers had married. They had not written and neither had her parents and she was not sure whether her Gran could or would have had to get Squire to do it for her.

Peter Churston was taking Sam to the station in the car. She had said goodbye to Susan and Harry and to Charlotte and was ready with her bags when he came to pick her up. She shut the caravan door with a small sadness because it had been her home and castle and hers alone and she had been contented there. But it was not a job for life and time for her to move on. She thought with satisfaction of the note tucked away in her money belt, that Squire Thorn had given her for emergencies. She did not need it to get home as he had suggested but it had been a support and comfort to her.

Sam thought about the time when she had left home as she sat, gazing out of the window, in the train. She wondered, now, at her decision to walk over the moor when she was hardly in the peak of condition; she remembered the stops she had made but little of the actual walk when her mind must have been totally taken up with her situation and the events that had led to it. It would be beautiful, now, July just arrived, not the full, dry heat and dust of late July and August - and she would be home for her eighteenth birthday. Just two years since she had left school, eager to start on her new life. And what disaster had come within weeks.

It was not a long journey to Exeter and as she collected up her bags, she was looking forward to her first sight of her 'own moor' and wondering if she would be able to go and work for Briar Thorn again: now she had her driving licence and her assistant instructor's certificate she would be able to make a more valuable contribution - if they wanted her. She had the memory of Briar and her half-brother Dan Thorn in her mind as she walked along the platform so it was not a great surprise to see him at the exit.

"Hullo, Sam" he said. "Give me your bag."

"You meeting me, sir?" she said.

"Yes. Your Gran told me the time your train came in and as I had some business in Exeter I said I'd pick you up." He ushered her out of the station and across the road to his Range Rover.

"I've learned to drive now" she said. "And I've got my A.I."

"So I was told. Congratulations to you, Sam. You haven't wasted your time."

She climbed into the passenger seat and started to pull the note from her belt.

"I didn't need this" she said. "But it was a great comfort having it."

Dan Thorn glanced down and smiled.

"Keep it, Sam" he said. "It is your talisman."

They had driven for a while without talk, she with her eyes seeking glimpses of the moor as they went along, he content to leave it to her to speak when she wished. She did, as a thought struck her.

"They're all right at home, ar'n't they?" she asked.

"Yes. But there have been one or two changes. Josh and Linda have got married." He paused.

"Is Nat still there?"

"Yes."

She nodded. She supposed Nat would have her room while Josh and Linda had what used to be the boys' room.

"You're taking me back to Gran's, then" she stated.

"What are you planning to do?" he asked. "Or have you not thought, yet?"

"Not really. I wondered, now I got my exam., if I'd be useful to Miss Thorn."

"You don't want to go further afield, then? Like Ben and Beth.?"

"Would they have a job for me?" she asked, eagerly. "I'm eighteen soon and I could learn to drive a box."

He laughed, gently.

"We'll see" he said and she knew he was not ready to say more.

Because they were going to Stony Gravel Lane and not to Bellacombe, she was not surprised when they took the upper road from Moorcombe though she was sorry not to go along the moorside road. But she was startled when he pulled up on the stretch of green beside Thornwood Church and got out.

"Come, Sam" he said. "We'll stop here, first."

She went with him, through the iron gate to the churchyard, glancing at the headstones as they went. She saw one inscribed to Daniel Carloss and to Annys, his wife. She saw the tall cross to Adam Thorn and his wife and, nearby, one to Anthony and another newer, to Columb Thorn, Air Commodore, RAF and then Squire Thorn's hand was on her arm and she looked at a new white headstone which said 'To the Memory of Reuben Lee, aged 47 years and of his son, Samuel, aged 3 days.'

She contemplated this solemnly, wondering if she was really surprised. Then she looked up at Thorn.

"Li'l tacker died, then" she said. "But Da?"

"He fell in the river."

Sam nodded.

"He drowned himself. Why are they buried here and not at Lydston?"

"Your Gran was bringing the baby here- and Nat wouldn't have your Da back home. So your mother has come to live here in the cottage and has let the boys have Bellacombe."

Sam considered this, gravely.

"There won't be room for me at the cottage" she said.

"No. You will come to Firethorn for now. All right?"

"Yeah." Sam looked down at the grave. "Samuel. Poor li'l tacker."

Chapter 14

Briar Thorn came into the room where her half-brother sat at his desk and cast herself into the armchair in front of him. Dan, looking up at her with humorous affection could still see in her the pugnacious red-headed child who had stood outside the stables and bawled for her pony while he lay in the hay loft and, unseen, looked down at her, standing in the sunlight.

"The girl's dead" she announced. "Numb. She can't still be in shock, surely?"

"Could be. Perhaps she should have stayed and faced it out."

"And seen her father drowned? Her mother kicked out by her brothers?"

"Yes. It could have snapped her out of it. But she went away - did lots of things - learned a great deal - and buried her feelings."

"She didn't know the child was dead - and buried - before she left?"

"No. Reuben, too. So she wouldn't have seen it. But it would have been here for her to face if Kezia hadn't packed her off."

Briar ruminated.

"She's been here a week. She's a good worker. A lovely

rider. But we don't need her here and she knows it. The Lindells need help. What about that?"

Dan met her eyes.

"You know the situation there. It could be a good thing. Her own mare is there, too. Get on to Cris and see if he agrees."

"Yes, OK." Briar paused. "You don't think Ashgrove is a bit near to Bellacombe?"

"Sam's no quarrel with her brothers, has she? She can't avoid them for ever."

Briar got up, still hesitant about her idea.

"Wonder what Celia Lindell will think. I'll go and call Cris."

Cris came to the Firethorn stables that afternoon and Briar left him and Sam in the sunlit yard together.

"I thought you might have come to see Dream by now" he said. "Have you seen your brothers?"

Sam shook her head.

"So much has changed - from what I was expecting" she said.

"Nothing is as you expect it to be when you come back. But you knew about your father and little Samuel, didn't you?"

"No. Gran never wrote. They've been putting the money I sent for - him - away for me." She gave a little laugh. "I'm quite rich."

"You don't want to buy Dream back?"

"No. I couldn't keep her here. I must find a job. I thought there might be one with Ben and Beth But I just needed some time to - get settled."

"Would you come and work at Ashgrove? I'm too busy with the estate so I've either got to get a secretary or a groom - and it would be great to know that the horses are decently looked after."

Sam regarded him, thoughtfully.

"How many you got?"

"Only three. Harry - Hereward the Wake, you know - and Dream and a new youngster."

"Harry" she murmured and wondered how the little boy was and how he was adapting to being his father's heir in place of his elder brother. "Yes - OK, Cris. Have you any further plans for your stables? Where do I live?"

"You'd better come and see Mother and fix something" he said.

Celia Lindell looked at the girl, noting the fine bone structure of her face, the dark curls, still fairly short-cut and the steady eyes.

"There's just myself and Cris here, Sam" she said. "I think the best thing would be if you live in the house 'as family'. It would be silly to have separate meals and so on, don't you think?"

"Yes. I lived as family with Simon and Melissa Randall so I - " She paused, regarding Mrs. Lindell, considering how best to put it. Straight, she decided. " - I know how to go on, fairly well."

Celia laughed.

"I'm sure you do. Anyway, we're not very formal and you will soon pick up our ways."

So Sam moved in to Ashgrove House and on her first morning she and Cris rode down the road towards the moor and along the lane to Bellacombe.

"Go in and see your brothers, Sam" said Cris. "I'll ride on quietly and you can catch me up."

It was strange, riding into the yard of the home that was no longer hers, that no longer had either of her parents within - Reuben buried with baby Sam and Becca over at Thornwood with Gran'ma Kezia.

A woman, heavily pregnant, came out of the central door and Sam had difficulty in recognizing Linda. Behind

her came Nat and it struck Sam that Linda may have
married Josh but was probably wife to both brothers.

"We 'eard you was back" said Linda. "Over to
Thornwood be yu, wi' yer Ma?"

"Hullo, Linda." Sam was suddenly conscious that her
year away, in the company of the Randalls, the Moxons
and the Churstons, had taken away her accent and the way
of speech that she had used at home, if not at school. "I
heard you were married. How are you, Nat? How's Josh?"

"We'm fine. Ma's told you we got Bellacombe, now?"

"Yes. Any ponies?"

"A few. Mainly cattle and sheep, now. You back wi' that
Briar Thorn again?"

"No. I'm working for the Lindells. This is Just My Dream
I'm riding."

"What Da gave yu an' yu sold" jeered Nat.

Sam, totally alienated, nodded.

"Well - sorry not to see Josh" she jerked and turned to
ride away.

Linda and Nat stood at the doorway and watched her go,
his hand on her shoulder. Sam wondered whose child she
carried.

The sky was overcast and the moor looked bleak and
empty as she rode out of the gate from the lane. She paused
after shutting the gate and looked up towards the tors. Was
it still her beloved moor or had it cast. her off, believing
itself deserted? Would it mean the same to her as it always
had, now that she had been further afield, seen and known
another moor?

The clouds were moving fast and broke apart, letting
through a shaft of sunlight that spread over the summit of a
Tor and widened, turning the coarse grass and bracken to a
golden sea. Sam drew a deep breath and took up her reins.
In the distance she could see Cris and Harry and she trotted
up the gravel track and on to the grass where she put

Dream into an easy canter. Harry turned and Cris sat quietly, waiting for her as she cantered towards him.

It was Sam's birthday early in July, her eighteenth birthday. She could remember how pleased she had been that her sixteenth birthday came before the end of term so that she did not have to go back to school after the summer holidays. She did not think of what happened in those holidays.

She had said nothing about it to Cris but found birthday cards and a dressage whip from him and his mother at her place at breakfast.. Then she and Cris rode over to Thornwood and stopped at the cottage in Stony Gravel Lane where her mother and Gran had small gifts for her.

Then, during the afternoon as she was cleaning the saddles and bridles they had used, in the tackroom, a horsebox drew up in the yard and Cris came in followed by Ben and Beth Thorn, both bubbling over.

"Hullo, Sam" said Ben. "Nice to see you, again. We've just come from the Croft. The Major and Mrs. Moxon sent their kind regards and Liz sends her love. Come and help us unload, will you?"

She went out with them and Ben lowered the ramp and opened the inner door. Placidly turning his head to look at them stood old Floristan.

"Oh!'" gasped Sam. "Is he coming here?"

"Happy birthday, Sam" said Beth "The old boy was retiring from school work and Dan thought you might like to have him for your own."

Speechless, Sam glanced at Cris and he nodded, smiling. "There's a box ready" he said. "See to him!"

Sam went up the ramp and caressed the gelding's neck, untied his headcollar rope and led him proudly down and into the stable. When he was settled and viewing his new quarters over the half-door between mouthfuls of hay, Sam turned to Cris.

"May I go and telephone Mr. Thorn? It is from him - my present?"

"Yes, of course" said Cris, answering both questions. "Beth - Ben - come in for some tea."

Dan Thorn answered the telephone and gently turned off her stammered thanks.

"You must have something to call your own, Sam" he said. "And taking Dream back would not be the same, would it?"

Sam recognized the truth of that and went into tea where Ben and Beth were telling Celia and Cris Lindell of their visit to the Croft School and on the table was an iced birthday cake with a key on it and 'Sam, 18' in pink letters.

"Are you coming of age, now, Sam?" asked Beth "Or waiting till you are 21?"

"I think I'm well of age now" said Sam. "I qualified, I learned to drive, I've got a horse and now a beautiful cake. Thank you, everyone."

She found the routine at Ashgrove to be simple and informal. They had meals in the breakfast room which was half the size of the dining-room. Each got for themselves what they wanted for breakfast - cereal, toast, egg, tea, coffee, orange juice and Sam was usually down first to put the kettle on the Aga. Cris followed and Celia Lindell a little later. A pause for coffee mid-morning, a scratch lunch on weekdays, another pause for a cup of tea mid-afternoon, and then Celia prepared supper. On Sundays they reversed lunch and supper and had a good roast lunch and a light supper. Celia went out on occasion in the evening to a meeting in the village or to visit friends and it did not take Sam long before offering to prepare the meal to save her from putting it ready for them, earlier. She began to do it occasionally when Celia was home and was rewarded when she was complimented on her dishes and told how nice it was to be cooked for sometimes - like Melissa, thought Sam.

She had a big, sunny room, overlooking the stable yard which she kept clean herself, although a 'daily' came in from the village to clean the house, each weekday morning.

The four horses in stables kept her happily busy and Cris managed to ride out with her most days. She practised her dressage on both Floristan and on Dream who was coming on nicely but enjoyed riding out on the moor. Cris soon turned his youngster over to her for schooling and rode Harry, generally. On her free days, Sam rode over to Firethorn and left her horse there while she helped Briar, lunched with them and visited her Ma and Gran'ma. It was a fine, peaceful Summer.

Chapter 15

Having for so long, at school, considered Cris as very much her senior, it took a little while for Sam to realise not only that he was still only twenty but also that she was very much the more mature.

He worked hard on his Estate duties but was guided by his Trustee and would be until he was twenty-five and Celia did a great deal to help with correspondence and in talking with the more difficult tenants. However, he took his position seriously and served on the parish hall committee and read the lessons, in turn, in Church.

Sam wondered how long he could be content, exercising his horses, hunting in winter, attending to his duties, living at home with his Mother, taking an annual holiday in Scotland or Wales or abroad. She thought of Benedict Thorn who had gone to Germany for five years when he was eighteen to concentrate on his dressage training. Cris should have gone to university, she thought: three years away from home would have done him good. He had been to boarding school, of course. She couldn't see him taking to dressage but Hereward the Wake was a good strong eight-year-old. Perhaps eventing.

She spoke of her ponderings to Briar one day when she was over at Firethorn.

"I can't think he will be satisfied with what he is doing for the rest of his life" she remarked.

"Are you discussing young Lindell?" asked Dan, who had joined them. "I don't think he has your questing spirit, Sam. You'll see - he'll be a hunting, bucolic squire like his father and not ask for anything better."

"It satisfies you?" said Sam, doubtfully.

Dan's lips twitched but Briar laughed.

"Remember, Sam, we're of the war generation. I think Dan had his fill of travel and adventure before he came back home to settle."

Sam nodded. She had heard something of the war exploits of Thornwood's Squire but she was thinking of the picture raised by his remarks on Cris. She realised, slowly, that he could be right.

It would not be enough for her, she thought. But, if she stayed for, say, five years - and she was happy enough and comfortable enough at Ashgrove - she would be twenty-three and should have good knowledge and experience and be mature enough to be entrusted with travelling horses abroad. Perhaps, then, Ben and Beth Thorn would take her on – and they would take Floristan too since Dan had given him to her. She felt she had planned a reasonable future, insofar as anyone could plan. It was something to work for, anyway.

She sounded Cris one day as they came into the house for coffee after riding.

"Do you see your future stretched out quite happily in front of you?" she asked him.

"Yes, I think so" he said. "I always knew I'd have to take on the estate- it came a bit earlier than I wanted but it was just as well I didn't have to stick at university. I didn't really know what to read. I suppose I shall have to be thinking of getting married, sometime." He paused. "We're too young, yet, Sam but we get on well. I don't suppose you'd think of marrying me - ever?"

Sam, startled, sat down rather heavily at the kitchen table.

"Oh, Cris, no! No, you must see, I couldn't. You will want children to follow you. I can't have them. You'll meet someone when you're older. Let's just go on as we are."

She became aware of Celia who put down steaming mugs of coffee on the table.

"Sam. Dear Sam" said Celia and they both stared at her. She drew a deep breath. "I want you both to come with me for a moment."

They followed her to a passage at the rear of the house and into a sort of utility store-room. There were some old pictures stacked by a wall and Celia turned one to the light and let them stare at it. It showed a dark-haired woman with a delicate boned face, with dark eyes and warm, brown skin.

Sam said, slowly "It's a bit like Ma but it's more like me."

"It is you" said Cris, disbelievingly.

Celia led the way back to the kitchen and sat down with her coffee.

"That was your great-great-grandmother, Cris" she said. "Spanish, of course. Sam, you know your Mother was a very beautiful, striking woman when she was younger?"

Sam nodded, suddenly aware of what was coming.

"I was ill for some time after I had Crispin" said Celia. "And then they said it would be dangerous for me to have another child. John - sought his pleasure elsewhere - for a short while. He had a liaison with Rebecca and you, Sam, were the result. It brought him to his senses. Fortunately, Reuben did not suspect. He accepted you as his own. But the fact remains that you are Cris's half-sister."

Sam took a swig of coffee.

"Well - I reckon we've always had that sort of feeling for

each other" she said, steadily. "I've always had a sort of affection for Cris and he's always been kind of protective to me."

"And Rebecca was happy - with the situation?" asked Cris, doubtfully.

"Yes. She has been splendid. She knew I knew. She's never tried to make any difficulty and, of course, John made provision for her - and for you, Sam."

Sam, grinned, tension dropping away.

"Oh, I'm quite well off" she said. "But, Mrs. Lindell - what about you? It must have made you unhappy."

"I was only unhappy because I would have loved to have a daughter" she said. "I watched you growing up with those two louts as your brothers but I trusted Rebecca to protect you. And then, the unthinkable happened. Perhaps - that caused John's stroke. He was very proud of you."

Sam took Floristan after lunch and rode over to Firethorn. She thought confusedly over Celia Lindell's attitude, not understanding how she could accept her husband's child with another woman.

The stables were quiet when she got there and she put Floristan in a loose-box with a slice of hay and took off his tack. Then she walked down the back drive to Stony Gravel Lane. As she came out of the gates, she looked at the cottage across the now tarmac-covered road but she did not want to go there, yet. Her Ma - and Squire Lindell? At present she could not take it in. She turned up the road towards the church.

She was sitting on the grass beside the grave of Reuben and their son Samuel when Dan Thorn found her.

"I'm a bastard" she told him. "Like Sammy here."

"And he was not the result of incest" said Dan.

Sam considered this but went back to her doubts.

"How can Mrs. Lindell not mind that it was her husband - and my Ma?"

"Sam -your Mother was a very exotic creature twenty years ago. She has beauty still. Celia Lindell had just learned she could give John no more children. She may have felt a failure, that she was letting him down, even perhaps that she should leave him, let him re-marry to get more children. It could have been a relief - or a release - that he did - as he did. It was a brief affair. Your Mother recognized his need. But he loved his wife and she had given him a son. I think they were grateful."

Sam got up, slowly and stood before him.

"So - what am I now?"

"You are a lovely girl with a sound background and a life in front of you. You have health, education, skills and talents. Do you ask more?"

Sam regarded him for a moment with grave, speculative eyes. Then she looked at the inscription on the headstone.

"He was my son, too" she said. "Not my brotherson, after all."

Dan laughed.

"Come on" he said. "Come and see your Ma and Gran'ma."

She went with him down the church path. So much had happened, so much even to her Mother, so much more would happen. Life had to be lived.

No Roses

Chapter 1

The ship, ploughing through a moderate sea towards her home port, was not too badly damaged. A fire on the foredeck was under control and damage repair parties were busy patching holes. Astern, the enemy ship had sunk, leaving only debris on the surface of the waters. The three survivors had been picked up and were below in the sickbay.

On the bridge, the Commanding Officer with two and a half rings on the sleeve of his reefer jacket, cast a look around and handed over to the Officer of the Watch. With darkness approaching, danger was slight; the men had stood down from Action Stations and were hopefully enjoying a meal, possibly only of sandwiches and tea as most of the cooks and stewards had been acting as first aid parties.

The C.O. left the bridge and went below to the sickbay where the young doctor met him and they went round the casualties, offering comfort and encouragement where they could to the wounded men. One of the rescued men was the C.O.'s opposite number, as shown by the equivalent rings on his uniform and he lay unconscious in one of the cots, his wounds tended and bound, his lips moving occasionally as he muttered some indistinguishable words.

The doctor had the names of the survivors which had been reported when the outcome of the skirmish had been signalled triumphantly and the C.O. stood looking down now at the man he had defeated and wondered if, through the unconscious mind were passing some of the memories that they both shared.

They had met seventeen years ago in 1928. Lord Robert Trevane, standing foursquare in front of the great granite fireplace in the hall of his house together with his wife and son, was welcoming his errant sister and her child to his home. She was errant because nine years before, less than a year after the Armistice, she had met and married, in Egypt, Herr Jurgen von Metz who had turned out to be a German industrialist, partner with his father in a business on a par with Krupps, supplying steel for munitions, ships and tanks for the Kaiser's forces. Now, even more errant, she was divorced and thereby disgraced and seeking shelter. Her elder brother had succeeded their father as Marquis of Brent Haven and wanted nothing to do with her so she had come with her son to her second brother until she could sort out her life.

"How old is the boy, Annie?" said Lord Robert, glowering on them.

"He is eight" said she who had been Lady Anne Sophia Trevane, now Frau Anna von Metz.

"Well, you'd better get him out of that rig" said her brother. "He can have some of Roddy's things to go on with. What's his name?"

"Gerhard" said Anne, resignedly because she had put this in the letter when she had first written to Robert and Lucy.

The child stood impassively, a small figure with cropped fair hair, dressed in lederhosen with embroidered H-braces over a white shirt and white knee socks. Beside his mother, ten-year old Roderick Trevane eyed the newcomers and thought that at least the boy would have things that he had long grown out of, considering the difference in their sizes. He was a robust boy with dark hair and a tanned skin wearing grey flannel shorts to his knees with a shirt and pullover. He had been a boarder at his prep.school for a year now and was just home for the Summer holidays. He wondered if this boy would have meals in the dining-room to which he had been promoted on starting boarding-school or be relegated to the nursery with six-year old Melanie under the care of Nanny Stanton and the nursemaid. Aunt Annie, he thought, looked a dowdy drip, with an almost ankle-length fawn coloured skirt and matching cardigan and a beige cloche hat. Edgar, the footman, had taken her dustcoat and the luggage from the car which had brought them from the railway station and Ransome, the butler, was bringing in some tea to refresh them after the journey.

Lady Robert, her fingers negligently twisting the long rope of jet beads that hung down to her waist, watched the butler arrange the tea tray on the low table beside her and the parlour maid place the cake stand nearby.

"Roderick, darling" she said. "Take the little boy up to Nanny. He can have tea in the nursery."

Gerhard, whose eyes had gone hopefully to the cakes, looked up at his mother. She gave him a brief nod and he turned to follow Roddy.

"You do speak English then?" said Roddy as they went up the back stairs.

"Yes."

"Where do you come from?"

"We came from our house in Berlin."

"Have you got another house, then?"

"We have a house near Essen and, also, for holidays, near Konigsberg."

Roddy digested this. Not quite the penurious cousin he had been led to expect.

"Are you sorry to leave them?"

"Yes. I had my boat to sail on the Baltic. Are there boats here?"

"Yes."

They had reached the nursery wing on the third floor now and Roddy crossed the landing and opened one of the doors. The day nursery was a big room with well-worn and comfortable old furniture. Against the grey July day outside it had a cosy air and, for a moment, Roddy regretted that he had left its shelter. Just sitting down to tea at the large circular table in the centre of the room, were Nanny Stanton, a stout woman of some fifty years and Melanie, a pretty, dark-haired child, being served by the nurse maid.

"Well, Master Roderick and what do you want?" said Nanny.

"This is Gerhard" announced Roddy. "Mother says he is to have tea up here. And Father said he's to wear some of my clothes."

"That's as may be. Jenny, take Master Gerhard to wash his hands and bring another cup and plate."

"Yes, Mrs. Stanton."

Roddy escaped and clattered down the back stairs again, hoping there was an eclair left for him. If not, he expected Cook would have some in the kitchen and she would not see him go without one of his favourite cakes. He decided to go straight to the kitchen. A cake there and a glass of lemonade seemed much more attractive than tea in the hall with his parents and Aunt Anne.

In fact, Anna von Metz was just gathering up her handbag and gloves to seek her room and Lady Robert, after offering more tea, rose resignedly to escort her there, leaving her in the charge of the maid who was engaged in unpacking the suitcases that had come with them. The trunks would be delivered by carrier later.

"If Master Gerhard is to be in the nursery wing, his clothes had better go over there" Anne said.

"Yes, m'Lady." Maria, the maid whose real name was Annabel - most unsuitable - had been instructed that Frau von Metz would be known as Lady Anne von Metz now she was home in a civilized country. "I'll send the nursery maid to collect them."

Gerhard, having finished nursery tea consisting of paste sandwiches and Victoria sponge with a cup of weak tea, had been set to play with Melanie. Fortunately, she was a lively child, getting him to repeat to her words in his own language which she picked up with the extraordinary facility of childhood.

He had not yet been stripped of his lederhosen, Nanny deciding that the change could quite easily be left until morning. She found she could approve of his quiet manners and patience with the little girl. That he was drained of energy by the three day journey and the misery of losing his homeland and all he held dear there, did not occur to her. He, mindful of his father's admonition that Prussians do not show emotion, kept his sorrow and weariness to himself. Until bedtime.

A brief skirmish with Nanny who had wished to supervise, resulted in him taking his bath alone; then, in pyjamas and dressing gown he joined Melanie for their supper of milk and biscuits and, at last, he found himself in a narrow, painted wooden bed, with the unaccustomed sheets and blankets in place of his own big down-filled coverlet, the dark oak door closed and the curtains drawn across the windows, dim shadows from the tall wardrobe and the heavy chest of drawers menacing him as he lay there. He was too tired and overwrought to sleep and yearning for all he had left behind and lost overcame him and the tears began to flow.

He did his best to muffle his sobs but misery took hold and he wept with fierce despair until the door opened and someone came in. He thought it might be his mother who usually came to bid him goodnight but it was Nanny who took him in her arms and hushed the choking gasps that wrenched his chest and stroked and soothed his wracked little body until sleep claimed him at last.

Below, Robert and Lucy sipped their sherry before dinner as they waited for Anne to appear.

"Why on earth did she marry him?" Lucy remarked, idly. "The magic of Egypt, passion by the Pyramids?

"She was twenty-nine" conceded Robert who was ten years older than his youngest sibling. "Perhaps she felt it would be her last chance."

"Did he divorce her or vice versa?"

"No. She divorced him. For adultery, I believe," said Robert, with distaste.

"One can hardly blame him. She's rather a depressing sort, isn't she?"

"She was not,, when she was younger." Robert looked back in his mind. "During the War, when I came back on leave, she always had plenty of young officers around. Good sport, played a good game of tennis, rode to hounds when they were still hunting. Seemed a bit lost after the Armistice. That's why Father packed her off to Egypt."

Lucy toyed with the idea of a lover killed in battle but before she could suggest it to Robert, Anne came into the room.

"Should I go and say goodnight to Gerhard?" she suggested. "He might be waiting for me."

"He'll be tucked up and asleep by now if I know Nanny" said Lucy with a glance at her watch. "Sit down, Anne. Sherry?"

Anne, slightly resentful of the way her son was being removed from her, sat down. Lucy might be the wife of a Marquis's younger son but her father, Sir John Burrows, was only a baronet. However, she had all the commanding forcefulness that the divorced wife of a commoner and a foreign one at that, could not display. No use to argue that Jurgen von Metz and his business interests already made it possible for him to buy up Robert's home and, indeed, their family home where their elder brother lived now, if he so wanted to make an offer. For herself, the divorce settlement and the allowance for the boy, made her quite independent. But for the present to live here at Hayle Manor on the Exe estuary was better for her than to be a lone woman, occupying a residence with her child and a chaperone.

She had come to dinner in a low cut, long sleeved gown, and a three row pearl choker which Jurgen had given her and at which Lucy looked sharply. Lucy was also wearing pearls having replaced her jet beads with another long rope which she had twisted once about her throat and allowed to hang just below her fairly ample bosom. She did not affect the flat-chested 'flapper' look of her sister-in-law.

"George's ship is coming into Plymouth next week" remarked Robert, as they settled to their soup. "I'll take the boys down. What about you, Anne? I know Lucy won't want to go."

"Oh, no" shuddered Lucy. "All those steep ladders - and the draughts:"

"Yes, I'd like to see George again" said Anne, placidly.

George was the third brother, two years younger than Robert and while both the elder boys had served during the War in Guards regiments, he had already chosen the sea as a career and had gone as a cadet at the age of twelve in 1894. He now had command of a cruiser with the rank of Captain. The remaining member of the family, a sister three years older than Anne was married to a Scottish laird who entertained Robert and Lucy and the Marquis of Brent Haven with his wife and eldest son for the grouse shooting in August.

Nanny had found some blue shorts and a sailor top in the luggage which Jenny, the nursemaid, had fetched for Gerhard and she had laid them out on the chair by his bed so after washing in the bowl of cold water that Jenny poured out for him on the washstand in his bedroom, the boy dressed himself in those, only too pleased to have his own clothes and not some of Roddy's outgrown ones and went along to the day nursery for his breakfast. A soft-boiled egg, toast soldiers and a mug of cocoa was fare for him and Melanie and then Nanny took them down to attend household prayers. After that he was allowed to go out to play with Roddy.

Roddy was quite pleased to have a male companion and decided to test him for value as a playmate. He was allowed a fair amount of latitude if he kept to the rules and presented himself punctually and in a clean condition at mealtimes.

"Let's go down to the river" he said and Gerhard nodded.

He had seen his mother briefly after the prayers and had greeted her politely. 'We do not show emotion in public.' She had kissed him on the forehead but already she seemed to be almost a stranger in this, her native land, among her own family. She had let him go off with Roddy without a word and he kept up with the elder boy stoically as they left the formal gardens of the house and plunged into woodlands, coming out on to coarse grassland bordering the estuary bank. But the tide was in, covering their stretch of foreshore and the mudbanks and there was only the dinghy tied up to the private jetty.

They stood on the bank, the sturdy, dark-haired boy and the slight blond one and looked at the water. The sea, coming up, had washed up some debris on the foreshore and was now leaving it behind. With the tide on the turn and the river flowing down to join it, the currents would be fierce. Used to the treacherous Baltic, Gerhard shook his head firmly when Roddy suggested they row upstream.

"For us, it would not be safe" he said and so decisive was his tone that Roddy accepted this without question.

Chapter 2

Until 1925, Lord and Lady Robert Trevane had driven to church, if the weather were poor, in the brougham. But in that year Robert was tempted into buying a large grey Bean with a fold-down fabric roof and mica side-screens which were stored in the boot until needed. The head groom and coachman was then able to take things more easily in his advancing years and the under-groom became a chauffeur.

However, as the first Sunday after Anne and her child arrived was fine and warm and the Church was just beyond the East gate, the family walked along the drive through the parklands, Robert and Lucy in the lead with Anne and Melanie behind and the two boys bringing up the rear. Both the boys were in grey flannel suits with kneelength socks, Roddy with his school boater and Gerhard with one of Roddy's grey flannel school caps. Melanie was unhappy in a flowered voile frock over a silk petticoat with white gloves and. a white straw hat.

The family went almost directly from their gate in through the lych-gate to the church and joined the people from the village around to the church door where most drew back to allow them to enter first. The Trevane pew was at the front, just below the pulpit and they filed into it in reverse order so that the boys were at the wall end and

Robert next to the aisle. All three children had their sixpenny piece to put in the collection plate when it came round, the boys' safely in their coat pockets, the little girl's tucked into a glove. She had not always stayed for the whole service. Until she was five, Nanny had come too and had taken her home before the sermon. Now those servants who wished to attend, came to the evening service but Nanny chose not to bother.

Robert, who possessed a moderate but tuneful tenor voice, soon realised during the first hymn and the Venite that there was little sound coming from the further end of the pew. He muttered to Lucy, next to him, "Tell those boys to sing". She passed the message to Anne over Melanie's head and came back with the suggestion that perhaps Gerhard would not know the tunes. However, the boys exchanged mutinous glances and as the Te Deum got under way it became apparent that a thread of silver had joined in, a treble clear and true as a bell. Roddy, rising to the challenge, also produced more than his usual bashful mumble and proved that he had inherited his father's ear if not quite having the same soulless purity of his newly-arrived cousin.

Sunday dinner was a reversal, a cooked meal at one o'clock with a cold supper in the evening to enable cook and her minions to go to church. The children also attended the one o'clock meal although Melanie and Gerhard had nursery tea as their last meal, apart from the milk and biscuits after their baths.

Sunday afternoon, for the children, was spent in quiet occupations though the grown-ups were experiencing change in their routine. It was becoming fashionable to have Sunday tennis parties and to exchange the formal Sunday dress for white flannels and pleated tennis skirts which showed quite a lot of calf.

The day of the expedition to Plymouth to go aboard

Uncle George's ship dawned fine and warm. Miller, the chauffeur, who had been Ted the undergroom, brought the Bean round and Anne and Robert took their places on the back seat with Gerhard between them while Roddy had the joy of sitting in the front. His pleasure was somewhat dimmed by the fact that Gerhard was wearing a white sailor suit with long trousers and a sailor hat with a tally-band bearing 'SMS König' in gold letters and long tails down the back. Nanny had tried to replace it with one of Roddy's old ones with the inscription 'HMS Victory' but Gerhard had resolutely refused to let her change it.

They left behind a sullen Melanie who in her best clothes was to go with her Mother in the brougham and take the sea air in Exmouth.

At Plymouth, they found the ship riding at anchor in all her glory and had to wait on the dockside until a smart picquet-boat steered by an equally smart little midshipman came to pick them up. It was steam-propelled and the highly-polished brass funnel was a credit to the crew. They had about half a mile to go and Roddy, going green and white but managing to contain himself, was chagrined to find that both Gerhard and Aunt Anne had their sea-legs and showed no discomfort. Nor did Lord Robert, but Roddy could not have imagined him doing any other.

They mounted the accommodation ladder to the quarter-deck where Gerhard saluted with all the unself-conscious aplomb of the seasoned sailor and there and then Roddy decided on his future.

Lord George, amused, greeted his brother and sister and looked down upon his nephews benignly.

"Are you going to join the Navy?" he asked.

"Yes, Uncle" said Roddy and "Yes, Captain" said Gerhard.

They were handed over to a Chief Petty Officer, a bosun's mate who, they learned, was known as the Chief

Buffer, for a tour of the vessel while Robert and Anne went below to the Captain's quarters for a welcome drink.

After a wide-eyed round of the 'working parts' of the ship and the crowded mess-decks, the boys were collected by the Sub-lieutenant who held sway over the gunroom and were taken to wash and 'refresh' themselves, given a glass of orange juice each and handed over to the Captain's Secretary, an awesome being with two gold rings on his sleeves, divided by the white cloth of the Paymaster Branch. Bearded sailors, marine sentries and the short-jacketed snotties dazzled their eyes as they were shepherded aft to join their respective father and mother in the spacious quarters of their magnificent uncle.

The ship's executive officer, a Commander and the Secretary remained with them for lunch in the day cabin and Roddy noted with some surprise how vivid and lively his supposedly dowdy Aunt was in this company. The boys were expected to get on with their meal quietly and speak only when addressed but Uncle George had seen the German tallyband on Gerhard's cap, which was now sitting on the table in the lobby in company with the Commander's and the Secretary's caps.

"Can you tell me anything about the König, boy?" he asked during a lull in the conversation with his brother and sister, who were seated on his either hand.

"She fought at Skagerrak - what you call Jutland. In October 1918 two of her officers were killed and her Captain badly injured in Kiel, by Communist mutineers. In June 1919 she was scuttled in Scapa Flow." The clear young voice gave the details precisely and without emotion.

Captain Lord George Trevane regarded him for a moment, caressing his neatly trimmed dark beard.

"Yes. You know your facts" he said. Later, in the Captain's

private heads, he remarked to Robert "You've got a proper little Jerry, there, Bob."

"He and Roddy get on very well" said Robert. "By the time they've been to school together, he'll want to follow Roddy to Britannia"

"Going to make an Englishman of him, are you? What about Metz? Won't he have a say?"

The brothers' eyes met and Robert shrugged.

"Will depend on the terms of the divorce, I suppose. He was the offending party."

They left it at that and soon it was time for Roddy to steel himself for the return trip in the picquet-boat. He was thankful that once again he managed to survive without loss of dignity.

Gerhard, stripped of his nautical finery by Nanny on his return to the nursery, was pounced upon by Melanie, eager to hear everything he could tell her about the visit to the cruiser. He detailed the tour meticulously, describing the engine room and the gun-power as well as the cramped mess-decks, the gunroom and wardroom and the bridge with its navigational aids. Drinking it in avidly, she was too young to appreciate the precision of his observations.

The Summer Holidays progressed, day following what, in memory, became ever sunlit day. The boys played on the beach, rowed on the river, were sometimes allowed to take Melanie with them on carefully restricted outings. In August, Lord and Lady Robert departed for Scotland and Melanie joined her brother and cousin more often under the less tight supervision of Lady Anne and Nanny Stanton. In September, Roddy returned to his preparatory school and Gerhard joined Melanie at the 'Dame' school on the outskirts of Exmouth where the Headmistress wore sprigged navy-blue dresses to her ankles and shoes with a buttoned strap over grey lisle stockings. The dresses were long-sleeved and high-collared and she wore pince-nez on a fine chain attached to her bosom with a small gold safety-pin.

In October the two children rode out with Anne and sometimes went cub-hunting and when Robert and Lucy left again to spend some weeks at their London house, Anne opted to remain in Devon. It was an idyllic time and she could forget the stigma of being a divorcee.

In November, Gerhard was introduced to the Guy Fawkes Day fireworks and observed the Armistice Day two minutes' silence for the fallen of his mother's country. On St.Nicholas's Day Melanie was thrilled with the presents for children, a German custom of which Anne saw no reason to deprive her son.

Lucy and Robert were still in London and Roddy had not yet broken up from his school. Nanny Stanton was a bit wary of the foreign custom but decided it would not hurt to have a nursery Christmas tree and celebration some three weeks early. Far from Roddy's first estimation, she found Lady Anne to be a lively and stimulating presence in the absence of the formally-inclined Lord and Lady Robert. The two younger children thrived on their outings, riding and walking with Anne and Nanny felt it would have been good for Roddy. It also gave her more time and she began gradually to slip into the role of housekeeper. Fortunately, she and Cook had always enjoyed a good relationship with none of the more usual bickering between nursery and kitchen.

A week before Christmas, Robert and Lucy came back to Hayle with Roddy whom they had collected from school on their way down to Devon. On the morning of Christmas Eve they departed again, with a very reluctant Roddy, to spend the festive days at the family home of Brent with the eldest brother William and his Marchioness. They did not take Melanie because William's children were all out of the nursery now and it would have meant taking Nanny and having special nursery meals; and they could not take Gerhard because William would not receive his mother.

Anne was relieved. She had never got on with her eldest brother and was not sorry to remain at Hayle. She was also glad of the absence of Robert and Lucy because Jurgen had sent his son a beautiful scale model of the German Navy's four-masted sail training ship. He had also sent her a gold pendant in the form of the ancient Aryan symbol, supposed to represent the sun, a cross with arms of equal length, each having an equal extension at right angles: it had been adopted by the militant new political party formed in 1919 and she was certain that Robert would not approve if she wore it. For herself, she was quite attracted by the paramilitary parades they put on, the young men looking very smart in their brown shirts and breeches and boots with banners of blood red bearing this symbol in black on a white circle. She put the pendant away in the bottom of her jewel box but approved of Gerhard displaying his model ship on the dressing chest in his bedroom.

She took both children to the traditional carol service, took them for a long walk before their Christmas dinner of turkey and plum pudding, had nursery tea with them and a splendid iced cake and let them have their milk and biscuits in their dressing gowns by the big, decorated tree in the hall in front of the blazing log fire.

"I wish Roddy had been here" sighed Melanie, blissfully, as she went up the back stairs to bed and Aunt Anne tucked her in and kissed her goodnight before going to do the same with her son.

She took them to the Boxing Day Meet and they stayed out for an hour and a half before coming back to wolf down cold turkey and ham and bubble and squeak followed by mince-pies and Devon cream.

Roddy, returning with his parents two days later after his grown-up Christmas soon had his superiority knocked down by Melanie's ecstatic account of the time she and Gerhard had enjoyed. He resolved, inwardly, that he would stay, next year.

But Anne was not only brightening the children's lives. At the end of January Robert found himself hosting a Hunt breakfast and riding to hounds afterwards while Lucy entertained those who had stayed behind. By March, Robert was fully involved with the local Point-to-Point races and Anne and Lucy were forming a branch of the newly founded Pony Club. But world events were moving and not many years remained of their settled existence.

Chapter 3

In 1929, the industrial world crashed.. Robert found his income from investments was cut, unemployment made any increases in rental almost impossible except to the hardest hearted of landlords. Anne's contribution to the household was most useful. Her allowance continued to arrive although the newspapers wrote of hard times on the Continent. Even so, in September, Gerhard joined Roddy in boarding at the Prep. school. This time, he did take on Roddy's outgrown kit.

When Melanie asked if he would mind boarding he laughed.

"No! I shall be able to read my letters from Vati without Mother getting them first!"

The fact that he still used the affectionate diminutive for his father taught him an early lesson at the school. The boys heard it with a delighted hoot of laughter.

"Vati! Metz has got a farty father!" they carolled. He never used the word again. At the height of the recession in the summer of 1931, when Britain struggled to remain on the gold standard, all services were ordered to cut pay. The Admiralty decision to cut all rates by a shilling meant that the lower deck lost 25% of their pay, the officers only 11%. The Army and Air Force were being cut by only 10%. This led to the mutiny, in September, among ships of the Atlantic Fleet at anchor at Invergordon resulting in many mutineers being discharged and seven captains relieved of their commands. Perhaps closer to his men in a cruiser, rather than in a bigger ship, Captain Lord George Trevane was able to control them and retain his position.

The fact that, within a month or two, Japan commenced her lengthy war with China, passed more or less unnoticed in Britain but was not lost on Germany's rising leader, Adolf Hitler nor on Italy's Mussolini.

Their meeting took place at about the same time that Cadet Roderick Trevane dressed in his naval finery and prepared to depart for HMS Britannia, the training college at Dartmouth. Melanie and Gerhard watched him go off in the Bean with his father, their eyes wide with envy and admiration.

"Are you going there, too, Gair?" asked Melanie and the boy nodded, determinedly. In the meantime he returned to school, without the protection of his older cousin.

It was not always easy. Suspicions still lingered from the Great War, Hitler was an unknown quantity, not as yet in power; both Germany and Italy were re-arming although Britain held back for several more years.

At Dartmouth, Roddy was being initiated into the ranks of the lowest form of life in the Navy. But they had a burly nursemaid to help them sling their hammocks and stow their sea-chests - which must not be locked - and as he was a calm-tempered boy, ready to adapt and deal with whatever came his way, Roddy got by very well. He was a good average at his studies, useful at sports and could put on a broad Devon accent to divert any difficult situation amongst his peers and immediate superiors in his term.

Roddy was enjoying himself and not finding any reason to regret his decision to follow his Uncle George's example. The fact that he had an uncle who was a senior officer in the Service and who had been promoted to Rear Admiral in the half-year's Commissions and Warrants List did him no harm at all. He went home on Christmas leave and no-one, this year, went to Brent. He told them stories of life at Dartmouth, in front of the blazing fire with the candle-lit, decorated tree standing tall in one corner. But he kept his most intimate tales for Gerhard when they snatched time together in his bedroom, cross-legged on the counterpane. He told him of the officers and instructors, the other boys, the senior terms and the awe-inspiring Cadet Captains and they discussed the time when Gerhard would come to join him though they would only have a year together and for some of the time Roddy would be away on his training cruises.

That Spring of 1932, with both the boys boarding at their respective establishments, Anne accompanied her brother and sister-in-law to spend some weeks at the London house. It was at a Regimental Reunion dinner and dance that she met Major Henry Greville, who had been a junior subaltern with Robert and now, a man of some forty-five years, was at the War Office. He was also a Devon landowner, a widower with a family estate near Exeter.

He drove over one Summer evening when they had returned to Hayle to dine with them. All three children were at the meal, Melanie at ten being judged mature enough to join them but they retired after the pudding, saying polite Goodnights to the grown-ups. Lucy and Anne remained to have cheese and biscuits and fruit and one glass of port before withdrawing and Robert and Greville settled down with cigars to discuss the situation of the nation.

I shall have to get rid of the London house" Robert said. He had already, a year ago, sold the brougham and the carriage horses and pensioned the old coachman.

"Not a good time to sell, is it?" said Greville.

Robert shrugged.

"Depends on how long I can afford to keep it" he said.

"We're going to have to start re-arming soon" said Greville, abruptly. "Germany's building three battleships up to the limits agreed - if not over, if I know them. We don't know much about this Hitler fellow yet but he seems to have quite an army of these Brownshirts."

"Is re-armament going to help the recession?" queried Robert.

"It'll get steel production moving again. And put the shipyards back to work." Greville drew on his cigar and shifted his seat a little self-consciously. "I might be relieving you of one of your responsibilities, too. I'm going to ask Anne to marry me - if she'll have me." He gave a little laugh at Robert's surprise. "We're a bit long in the tooth now, I suppose but we've both done it before. She's met my two youngsters and they get along well. In any case Walter is off to Sandhurst shortly and Frances to Switzerland, finishing school."

"What about young Gerhard?" said Robert, quietly.

Greville rubbed his chin.

"Ye-es. We'll have to talk about him. Wants to go to Dartmouth, I believe?"

They looked at each other for a long moment. Robert sighed and got up.

"We'd better join them" he said.

Greville's mother, a widow approaching seventy but very active, kept the manor house going with a staff of seven while her son was in London and her grandchildren at school. As Greville had told Robert the boy was about to embark on his Army career with his sights on a commission in the Guards and the girl to be 'finished' with a view to presentation at Court and a successful marriage - by which was meant not necessarily a happy one but with an eligible and preferably titled husband.

Anne was aware of these circumstances but she had not

related them to herself as yet and Greville's proposal, that evening, as they walked on the terrace in the Summer dusk, was not expected. She was silent for a while, considering it.

"I may be in line for a job on the Viceroy's staff in Delhi" he went on. It would mean promotion to half-Colonel and it was usually thought to be better if the senior officers were married but he refrained from so saying in case she felt it to be his reason for proposing to her.

"What about Gerhard?" she said, "He should be going to Dartmouth next year."

"They won't take him" said Greville, bluntly.

"Why not?" she flared. "He's the grandson of the Marquis of Brent Haven; his Uncle is an Admiral."

"He's a German" said Greville.

Anne stared at him in indignation but she was silenced. Her son was, indeed, of German nationality.

"I shall have to think, Harry" she said. "Will you give me some time?"

"Of course, old girl. No immediate rush" he assured her.

Robert had told Lucy of Greville's intention but they did not question the terrace walkers when they came in and Greville took his leave with unimpaired cheerfulness. As Anne seemed a little thoughtful, Robert rightly concluded that she had not yet accepted but had not refused.

Blissfully unaware of Greville's prediction of rejection, Gerhard spent the days of Roddy's leave riding, boating and swimming with him and saw him return to Britannia, confident that next year he, too, would have a uniform of blue and gold.

A letter from the Headmaster of the preparatory school requested Anne to visit him with the boy.

"Lady Anne" he said when he had welcomed her and seated her in his study. "I am happy to tell you that Gerhard passed the entrance examination for the naval college but, unfortunately, they have refused the application for him to become a cadet." He saw the colour drain from the boy's face as he stood at his mother's side and a stricken look blank his eyes but he showed no other emotion. The man felt a sudden intense pity for him. Lady Anne did not seem surprised.

"It is, I suppose, because of his father" she said, sadly.

"I expect the question of his nationality came into it" the Headmaster admitted.

"He has dual nationality" she said "But his father - ." She paused and the Headmaster understood. The Metz iron and steel works were on a par with Krupps and, despite the depression in Germany which was as bad as in England, both these great firms seemed to be flourishing under the patronage, it was said, of the rising political force, the ever-growing National Socialist Workers' Party.

Gerhard said nothing. He saw the future, as envisaged, wiped away, leaving nothing. There was a blank wall in front of him and he stared at it, understanding only that England had rejected him. He had not understood the deeper implications in his Mother's words. His father was German so he had been rejected. The only way forward then must lie in Germany.

Lady Anne was saying Goodbye and getting up. The Headmaster escorted them back to the door where Miller waited with the Bean. Gerhard said Thank you and Goodbye to the Headmaster and followed his mother into the car. She looked briefly at his stony, white face and found nothing to say.

Gerhard wrote two letters that evening. He had a small room away from the nursery wing now and was relatively secure from any interruptions. He wrote first to Roddy and, insofar as he was able to let himself go, opened his heart to the older boy and, possibly without realising it, revealed the depth of his disillusion and despair. Then he wrote a polite and rather stilted letter to his father to ask if he could return home.

He did not put them on the hall table, as usual, to go in the post bag but, in the morning, he walked down to the village to the little post office and stores and bought stamps and carefully put the letters into the box.

There was no immediate reply from Jurgen von Metz which relieved his son who feared the effect on his mother if she learned that he was asking to go back to live with his father. A letter from Roddy was passed secretly to him by the sympathetic footman, Edgar, who collected the post-bag and who was now married to Jenny, the nursery maid.

Roddy responded magnificently. He was suitably indignant, could not understand the rejection of the application by the College and, with insight perhaps beyond his years, omitted the usual lavish details of his nautical exploits. He was quite enthusiastic about the idea of going back to Germany where he would be able to come and visit the Berlin and Essen establishments and the holiday home at Konigsberg; perhaps, even, his ship would call at Kiel or Wilhelmshaven when Gerhard's ship was there. He did not doubt that Gerhard would be joining the German navy which, despite the recession was expanding and providing employment to the stricken workers of the big ship-building yards.

Gerhard went back to school in September and, at the half-term, attended the quiet ceremony at the Exeter register office and the reception at a hotel in the Cathedral yard afterwards, for the marriage between his mother and Lieutenant-colonel Henry Greville. When he broke up for the Christmas holidays, he was collected, not in the Trevane old grey Bean but in the shiny black Humber driven by Greville and taken to the Manor House at Narraclyst. He had been given no opportunity to say Goodbye to those at Hayle: no-one had told him he would not be going back there.

Chapter 4

The first time the church at Narraclyst heard the silver treble blending with the voices of the congregation, they were singing 'Praise the Lord for He is Glorious'. What they did not make out, for the church was well-filled and in good voice for a well-known tune, were the German words which the boy sang with fervour, the National Anthem of what he now knew was his country. Only Anne, next to him, heard the words and wondered.

He met his step-brother and step-sister that Christmas; Walter was nineteen and a Sandhurst cadet and Frances at seventeen had returned from her first term in Switzerland. They looked from lofty heights upon the slender, blond boy with the unsmiling mouth and secretive eyes.

The Trevanes came over to lunch on New Year's Day, before Roddy went back from his Christmas leave: Robert, Lucy, Melanie and Roddy; and the two boys found a quiet place to talk. Gerhard had received a satisfactory Christmas letter from his father which, while not betraying his request, making it all right for his mother's scrutiny, yet managed to convey that it would be granted. He did not know how but he trusted his father to accomplish it.

A few days before Gerhard was due to go back to school, Henry received his orders to take up his post on the staff of the Viceroy of India at the beginning of March. A five-week sea-trip meant that he and Anne had to start their preparations right away.

"What are you going to do about the boy?" Henry asked. after dinner, one night. "There will be no place for him in Delhi. He'll have to stay at school for the short holidays. Perhaps they'll have him at Hayle for the Summer."

Gerhard, about to come in to say Goodnight, stopped short as he heard Henry's question.

"He would hardly want to come here on his own" said Mrs. Greville in a tone that suggested she was not prepared to have him there despite her seven-strong staff.

Lady Anne Greville looked from one to the other, sensing their hostility. She wondered if she had erred in leaving her brother's household.

"I have not had the opportunity to speak with Gerhard" she said, slowly. "But I have a letter from Jurgen. He wants the boy back."

Both Harry and his mother, finding their objections unopposed, began to expostulate. Gerhard walked into the room.

"I will go back to Germany" he said, flatly. "You do not want me, here. The Royal Navy does not want me. I expect the Reichsmarine will take me."

The three of them stared at him. Anne went towards him.

"Gerhard, dearest." She spoke in German. "You want to go?"

"You say my father wants me. I want to go."

"How about the divorce arrangements?" put in Harry, hesitantly. "Do they allow him to have the boy - permanently?"

Anne turned to him.

"Oh, yes" she said, bitterly. "He was given 'control and custody' or whatever they call it, although he was the guilty party. But he let me bring Gerhard with me while he was a child."

"What's that Jesuit saying?" said Harry. "'Give me a boy until he is seven and I will show you the man'. Well, he had him till he was eight and now we know. He's German."

The boy stood stiffly. He hated them all.

"Please" he said. "I want to say Goodbye to Roddy before I go."

"We'll have to see if there's time. Anne, you'd better let the school know he won't be going back there."

They managed to find time not only to see Roddy but also to go to Hayle. There, Gerhard rushed up to his little room and rescued his model sail-training ship which had been deemed too difficult to pack when his things had gone to Narraclyst despite the fact that it had survived a journey from Berlin. He gave it to Melanie. At Dartmouth, they were allowed to take Roddy out to lunch in the full glory of his cadet uniform with the white twist on the collar. It was not wholly satisfactory as the boys had no time alone to exchange confidences and could only promise to write. There remained then only the final packing and labelling of trunks and suitcases, which were to go in the hold and which to the cabin. The luggage belonging to Colonel and Lady Anne Greville was sent on to Southampton to the P.& O. liner which would take them to Bombay while they took Gerhard to London where he was to join a cargo liner to Hamburg. His belongings were condensed into a suitcase: January was cold so he was wearing his flannel school suit and overcoat which left less heavy garments for packing.

The ship was due to sail in two hours' time and, as Harry and Anne had to get back to Southampton they did not board with him. From the deck, for one heart wrenching moment, he stood and looked back, a small, forlorn figure and Anne choked back her tears. Then he turned away and disappeared. 'We do not show emotion' - or as the British said, so Roddy had told him 'Keep a stiff upper lip.' He went to the cabin he was directed to by a steward and wondered what Roddy was doing at that moment. He wanted to cry but he controlled it: he was CO of his ship and he had to go to the bridge and con her from the harbour. He wrapped his overcoat about him again and went up on deck, keenly noting the other shipping and considering the manoeuvres required to ease away from the dock and turn to go out into the river. It was quite a disappointment to him when the pilot came aboard and two tugs took the ship out into the mainstream and tooted in farewell as she set off for the estuary and the North Sea.

Roddy was, in fact, doing what Gerhard had tried to do in imagination. He was taking his turn in being in command of one of the training pinnaces from the College. He was in his element and his quiet confidence and firmly given orders made the Instructor-Lieutenant take note of him. A popular boy, sturdily built and not one to trade on his relationship to the newly-promoted Rear Admiral Lord George Trevane.

On the black-sided freighter, making her way down-river, the Captain had noted the blond-headed boy on deck. It was too cold for many of his dozen passengers to venture up and the boy, his hair longer than when he had first arrived in England, was very noticeable, with his obvious keen interest in all that was going on.

"Who's that lad?" he asked his Chief Officer. "On his own?"

"Name's Metz" said the Mate. "Travelling alone. Father owns big iron and steel works in Essen."

"That Metz!" The Skipper looked again with renewed interest. "See if he'd like to come up here after we've dropped the Pilot."

So, as they picked up speed again and the pilot cutter turned back to the river, the Mate came up to the wheelhouse with the boy, whose cheeks were flushed with excitement and introduced him to the ship's Master.

"Gerhard von Metz, sir" he supplemented with a duck of his head.

"You looked very interested down there, Mr. von Metz" said the Skipper. "Are you planning a sea-faring career?" "Yes, sir. I am going back to be a Seekadett in the Navy." The burly man in Merchant Navy uniform looked kindly and understanding and he added, confidingly "I passed the examination for the Royal Navy but the College would not take me as I am only half-English."

"So you're going to join the German navy? English mother, boy?"

"Yes, sir. But I go back to my father now I am grown."

Master and Mate exchanged a brief glance. Broken home, broken loyalties. Poor child. Had they made an enemy by rejecting him?

"Well, have a look round, lad. I'll be going down to dinner, shortly. You can come with me."

"Thank you, sir."

There was no Captain's table, as such. Those of the passengers who were not groaning in their bunks under the onslaught of the North Sea, all sat at one table in the passengers' dining-saloon. The Captain presided on the first night and his officers on subsequent nights, if any. But they would only have one night at sea on this leg of the voyage, their second dinner, presided over by whichever officer was off-watch, would be taken as they proceeded up the 75 miles of the Elbe to Hamburg.

Most of the passengers had disembarked when Gerhard was sent for to go to the Captain's cabin. There, with some Port officials, was an elderly man in grey livery, whom he recognized from four years ago.

"Mr. von Metz" said Captain Bone. "Your father's

chauffeur has come for you. I am satisfied with his credentials. Are you?"

"Thank you, Captain. You are very good. Yes. How are you, Emil?"

"I am well, Mr. Gerhard. How you have grown!"

The boy, stiff-backed and stiff-upper lipped, shook hands with the Captain, bade goodbye to the other men there and, clinging with some desperation to his self-possession, left the cabin with Emil.

"Where is my father, Emil?" he asked as they stowed his suitcase in the boot of the big Mercedes-Benz.

"He is in Berlin - where we go now" said the man, unhappily. "It is a very important day, tomorrow."

It was January 30th., 1933, the day Adolf Hitler took charge of Germany as Reichs Chancellor.

The Mercedes-Benz arrived at the Metz house on the outskirts of Berlin in the early hours of the morning but the city was already abustle. Gerhard was met by his father's valet and taken up to his old room where, begging Nanny Stanton's pardon, he tumbled into bed, under the big down coverlet, unwashed and fell asleep at once. Emil, after his long drive and fortified by a quick tot of cognac in the kitchen, also sought his bed although he would need to be up again at his master's call in two or three hours' time.

Gerhard also woke early. There seemed to be a buzz in the air, a suppressed excitement that permeated the atmosphere. He went down to breakfast in his English school flannel suit with the grey shirt and striped house tie that matched the colours on the tops of his knee socks. He thought, briefly, of his last English breakfast of eggs and bacon, fried bread and tea, served in the saloon of the SS Longbow yesterday morning and accepted hot rolls with butter and jam and coffee from the manservant, again an old acquaintance from earlier years.

"Thank you, Paul" he said.

"Are you glad to be home, Mr. Gerhard?" said the man.

"Yes" said Gerhard, smothering a sigh. "Where is my father?"

"He is at the Rally" said the man, proudly. "He will be with the Fuhrer."

"Can I go to see the Rally?"

Paul hesitated.

"I will enquire" he said. He had no desire to take responsibility for the safety of the von Metz son.

Strauss, the valet, came to Gerhard.

"It will be difficult for any but an official car to be on the roads today" he said. "But if you wish to walk I will arrange for one of the outdoor men to go with you. How near you will get I don't know. Your father will not be back to lunch."

"Thank you. Please arrange it. I will be back for lunch."

The house was some four or five kilometres from the centre of Berlin but well before they got there, crowds blocked their way. There seemed to be never-ending lines of marching brown-shirted men, all carrying the blood-red banners with the black twisted cross on the white circle. Few people took notice of the slender boy with the dark blue overcoat covering his bare knees and his companion, the head groom in his breeches was of a piece with the breeches and boots of the marching men.

It was stifling, despite the cold; it was claustrophobic, it was mesmerizing. The man and the boy walked and stared, the thumping bands, the thumping feet dragging them along the crowded streets, the chants - a single voice crying 'Sieg' and a roar of 'Heil' from a thousand throats. For a while Gerhard was almost entranced.. Then he pulled himself together, imagining Roddy's cool voice of reason. He stopped.

"Let's get out of here, Heinz" he said. "Time to get home."

The man nodded, grimly and turned into a quiet side street.

"That's right, Mr. Gerhard" he said. "I can see trouble in all this."

The boy had his midday meal in solitary state. Afterwards, he went outside. The house stood in its own grounds with stables and outbuildings and he wandered around, refreshing his memory. He had gone back indoors to the warm sitting room where there were some current magazines when he heard his father arrive and the door opened.

Chapter 5

Jurgen von Metz was a tall man, not yet running to fat, with fair hair turning to grey, sharp blue eyes and a commanding presence. He regarded his son, as the boy got to his feet, with a critical look which gave way to a satisfaction, a certain pride and a faint exasperation.

"English schoolboy, eh?" he said, unconsciously echoing Lord Robert as he added "We'll have to yet you out of that gear! Come here, boy."

Gerhard advanced, tentatively holding out his hand, aware of the dark-haired woman just behind the big man. Jurgen took the hand, laughing and swept the boy into a close embrace.

"It's good to see you, my son" he said. "Now, you must meet your stepmother."

Frederica von Metz was also tall. She was slender almost to the point of thinness and her dark hair was drawn back into a knot at her nape from a centre parting, framing an olive skinned face and dark brown eyes. Gerhard learned later that she claimed a Persian grandmother and certainly seemed to have something of the exotic East about her. At the time, however, he merely acknowledged his father's introduction with a short bow over the hand she gave him to kiss. She smiled at his wary formality and exchanged a glance of shared intimacy with his father.

There were guests to dinner that night, members of the National Socialist Workers' Party who had just swept to power under their Leader, Adolf Hitler and his chief henchman, Hermann Goering who was to be the Air Minister by virtue of his flying exploits in the Great War when he had taken over the Red Baron's squadron after Richthofen's death. Some of them were still in uniform, after the Rally, some, like their host, in dinner jackets. Frederica appeared in a long black gown, high-necked and long-sleeved, which accentuated both her slimness and the curves of her long body and thighs. Gerhard had been unsure of what to wear but he put on his long-trousered blue suit which they had worn at school on Sundays, with a white shirt and navy tie and it seemed to meet with his father's approval. He was introduced to the company, four men in uniform, two without and two wives in long evening dresses.

"A splendid young Aryan!" remarked one of the uniformed men, jovially and not looking at the dark woman who was the second Frau von Metz. They were all indulging in pre-dinner cocktails or straight aperitifs and Paul offered a salver to Gerhard with a glass of watered wine. He took it thankfully, sipping it quietly in the background, noting the attitude of the two wives - quite well-dressed - towards the exotic Frederica.

The conversation centred on the day's events, the Fuhrer's speech from the rostrum, the paunchy, bespectacled Rohm, assertive Goering and the skinny, lame little runt, Goebbels.

Jurgen von Metz had a good chef and the seven course meal was accompanied by appropriate wines which flowed as freely as the talk did when tongues were loosened. The fourth course was a splendid pork roast with many vegetables and side dishes.

"You are not a believer in vegetarianism, then, Jurgen" quipped one man.

"I've nothing against vegetarians" retorted von Metz "Except that they tend to flatulence which rather lessens the pleasure of their company."

Gerhard did not understand the roar of laughter that greeted this until he later learned that Hitler was a vegetarian and suffered considerable digestive problems. He was following Paul's whispered advice not to take too much of each course and, so far, was keeping up quite well. The menservants seemed to be well-disposed towards him and even the stately butler was carefully monitoring his wine intake. When the three women of the party had withdrawn and he had sipped the thimbleful of port in his glass, Jurgen nodded to him.

"You may say goodnight, Gerhard" he said.

"Yes, father." The boy stood up, bowed his head to the company and walked, straight backed from the room. He had no wish to join the women so he went up to his bedroom. It was warm from the radiators and he did not think he would sleep so soon after so much food and drink so he sat down at his desk and started to write a letter to Roddy at the Britannia Royal Naval College, Dartmouth.

Roddy read it with understanding: the thrill of being invited to the bridge of the SS Longbow by Captain Bone, the pleasure of finding Emil, Paul, Strauss and the imposing butler Diedrich still there; not quite hiding the disappointment of not seeing his father until the following day and. then in company with the strange woman who had become his stepmother. The description of the marching Brownshirts and the dinner party afterwards brought a more serious look to Roddy's eyes. The man Hitler was said to be doing great things in pulling Germany out of the recession while Britain still floundered but it all seemed to be very militaristic. The five-year construction programme for Rader and his navy was well into its first year, including motor torpedo boats, destroyers and modern 6,000 ton light cruisers with diesels in addition to their main steam turbines, thus increasing their range. It was making the British navy think because there was no reconstruction programme in being, so far, for them.

For Gerhard, it was painting a rosy future. To have ships equal to the British navy and to serve in them was his dream. That the idea behind their construction might be to challenge the British ships did not enter his head.

Relations with his stepmother were ambiguous. Her general attitude to him was charming but he sensed she resented his presence so his feelings towards her were wary. She held soirees which were very popular among the Nazi leaders who came to the big house in their breeches and shining boots and filled it with their coarse talk and laughter. How she discovered Gerhard's voice he did not know but Jurgen arrived home one evening to the brightly-lit house to hear the silver treble singing the soprano part of Strauss's Voices of Spring and to find a well-oiled crowd, including Goering, swaying to its lilt and Frederica accompanying at the piano. He had a drink with the company, saw them off the premises and took his son to his study. It was a day in early Spring and time, he realised, to do something about the boy.

"Do you like doing that sort of thing?" he asked.

"No, Father. I would like to go to Konigsberg until I can go to the Naval academy."

Jurgen considered him. It was a good idea, he thought. The boy could have his boat, go to the local gymnasium, get away from his stepmother and her circle.

"Very well" he said. "I shall send you with Emil

tomorrow. There are sufficient staff there to look after you. You will behave yourself and cause no trouble."

So began what Gerhard was to look back on as one of the happiest times of his boyhood. The steward and his wife who looked after the house were known to him and did little to curb his activities. A new boat was procured for him and he and an old friend, the son of a local fisherman, spent hours sailing, exploring and learning to look after themselves and each other. On his thirteenth birthday that Summer, Jurgen came and brought with him Roddy, on leave, able to stay for a week and due to join a training cruiser on his return to the College. The three boys became more adventurous and achieved a trip across to Danzig and back to Konigsberg. Beyond warning them to have a care for their English visitor, Jurgen made no objection.

Summer over, Gerhard attended the gymnasium and also joined the naval Hitler Youth. He found himself in demand to lead their marching songs and learned the Forces' lament 'I had a Comrade' and the words to 'Wine, Women & Song' penned, surprisingly by Martin Luther: 'Who loves not Women, Wine and Song, Shall be a Fool his whole life long', Later he was to learn the Nazi anthem 'Tomorrow Belongs to Me' and the sad poem 'There are no Roses on a Sailor's Grave'. At that time they held no more meaning to him than choruses to be sung among a group of boys indulging in healthy and active pursuits and all, he hoped, leading to his goal of entry into the navy.

He grew, mentally and physically, while at Konigsberg, into a tall, slim and well-muscled boy, doing well academically. He went to Berlin for Christmas and realised that Frederica was looking upon him with more warmth than was fitting between stepmother and stepson. He neither liked nor trusted her and was glad to get back to school and his companions.

He did well at the local school. Because of the naval

base it was geared to the sea and his studies for the BNC examination stood him in good stead. He managed to get on a sail training course and hoped for the naval academy at sixteen. His fifteenth year was eventful in that March saw the Luftwaffe established under Goering and the keels of the new battleships, Scharnhorst and Gneisenau, were laid down - several months in advance of the Anglo-German naval treaty which permitted them up to 35% of the English fleet: June that year also saw U1, the first U-boat off the stocks, commissioned. And in September, at the Nürnberg rally, Hitler decreed that Jews were sub-human.

Except for the ship-building programme, most of this passed Gerhard by. He was not interested in Goering's Air Force and he had long been aware, like most of his peers in the Hitler Youth, that Jews and Slavs were looked upon as being different to ordinary people. It did not worry him: Lascars in the merchant ships, Chinese laundry-men in warships, were different too. Hadn't they all got their place?

He went on holiday again to Berlin at the beginning of 1936. When he went to order his new uniform from the naval tailors there, his father had told him to have a dinner suit made and now, a cold January evening, they were off to the ballet, a gala performance which most of the Nazi hierarchy would be attending and he was wearing his dinner jacket and braided trousers under his overcoat in company with his father, similarly attired and his stepmother in a long black gown with an opulent fur wrap.

In the foyer, Gerhard noticed a tall, blonde woman standing alone, a veritable Brünhilde, her golden hair swept back into a french pleat. She and Jurgen and Frederica exchanged polite words of greeting as they moved past.

"Who was that?" asked Gerhard for she looked vaguely familiar.

"Lotte Blickman" said Jurgen, briefly which Gerhard recognized as the name of an operatic diva.

"I would not have expected to see her here alone" remarked Frederica.

"She comes to the ballet to see which male dancer has the biggest bulge in his tights" said Jurgen coarsely and Gerhard, who had not really noticed on his only previous visit to a ballet, soon appreciated his meaning.

Afterwards, they again saw the Wagnerian blonde, still alone.

"Your escort has been detained, Gnadige Frau?" suggested Jurgen and when she assented, he added, smoothly "Let my son see you home. Gerhard, escort Madame Blickman - the doorman will get you a taxi."

Startled, the boy pocketed the money his father slipped into his hand and bowed politely to the statuesque woman. She accepted his escort with a gracious smile and told him where to direct the cab driver.

It was an imposing apartment block in Berlin-Dahlem and, bemused, he accepted her invitation to go in and paid off the driver. The apartment was mostly furnished and decorated in gold and white and she gave him coffee and brandy. He visited the bathroom preparatory to departing and when he came back she had released her hair from the french pleat and was wearing a flowing white velvet wrapper which opened to reveal long, white legs. She took him to bed and deprived him, deliciously, of his virginity. For some reason, as he slid into sleep, he remembered Nanny Stanton and his first night at Hayle.

As he took another cab home in the pale pre-dawn, he realised she must be Jurgen's mistress and they had arranged this between them.

Chapter 6

While Gerhard's introduction to manhood had taken place in luxurious circumstances, cushioned and soothed by the voluptuous blonde with the covert knowledge and approval of his father, Roddy's was in one of the higher-class brothels of Portsmouth under the guidance of the Gunroom Sub. This young gentleman had taken exception to the dark line of down on Roddy's upper lip and had ordered him to shave it off as he did not imagine the senior snotty could muster a full set (of moustache and beard) as yet. However, he must have thought it indicated Roddy's maturity and so kindly introduced him to the pleasures offered by the ladies of the night. Roddy relished the experience but found it a little too expensive to repeat too often.

In July of that year, the Spanish Civil War broke out and some little while later Roddy found his ship involved in company with German naval vessels in evacuating nationals. He stood at the foot of the brow, encouraging the ex-patriates on to the ship, speculating on the life they were being forced to leave and wondering what awaited them back in Britain. He noted those filing on to the adjacent German ship and wondered how 'Gair', as he and Melanie called their cousin, was getting on at his marineschule. He would have another year to go before he was old enough to be accepted into the Reichsmarine - recently renamed by Hitler as the Kriegsmarine.

"Mr. Trevane - how many more to come?" The Officer of the Day at the entry port broke into his reverie and he glanced back along the line.

"About twenty, sir" he called and looked across at the armed seaman on the other side of the brow.

"'Bout that, sir" confirmed the man and gestured to the hands who were humping baggage to get a move on. The German ship, astern of them, was ushering the last of their intake and the young officer on the quay nodded to Roddy before following them on board. The gangway was removed, mooring wires were cast off and with the minimum of fuss and a few brief orders, the ship moved away from the wharf and set off home.

Roddy was glad when he could follow suit and take up his position for leaving port. Inland he could hear heavy guns and there were airplanes overhead - German or Russian - but they were keeping clear of the evacuation ships. The sound of the guns was disturbing. Roddy was glad they were not active participants in the war and wondered what it could be like to be on the receiving end of the gunfire.

While Roddy was ruminating on the perils of war, Gerhard was sprawled on the coarse grass above the waters of the Bay and his boat was tied up to the small wooden jetty below. Jerzy Krepka, the fisherman's son who crewed for him, had a sister, Jelena, who was a year older than Gerhard and well developed for her age. He was realising that this was likely to be his last summer at Königsberg and he would miss her. She had already allowed him to exercise the knowledge he had acquired from Lotte Blickman upon her and they lay in the quiet isolation of the spot in sated contemplation of the coupling. It had been highly satisfactory. Jelena found Lotte's teaching far superior to the clumsy approaches she was used to from the boys of the fishing village. Gerhard found her supple peasant body more delectable than Lotte's ample flesh.

He had not had another intimate encounter with the operatic diva but he had been to hear her sing Wagner in Berlin, a performance which the Führer had attended. Hitler had paused to speak to Jurgen and Frederica in the foyer and had nodded to the boy whose voice had broken that year so he did not lead the singing at his Hitler Youth rallies now.

Roddy still wrote to him as he did to Roddy. His mother, Lady Anne Greville, was still in India and wrote occasionally to tell him of life there and of the Viceroy's palace. Lord and Lady Robert sent him a card at Christmas and on his birthday and so did Melanie. She was now fourteen and at boarding school. Also, at Christmas, he received a card from his Uncle George, now Vice-Admiral Trevane, to whom he dutifully responded, sometimes with a twinge of regret that he would never come under that respected officer's command. His eldest uncle, Lord Brent Haven, kept sternly aloof and so did his Aunt, Lady Alexandra Campbell, married to the Scottish laird. On his father's side, he had no known relatives: Jurgen had been an only child and his parents were dead. Any siblings of theirs were not in touch with him or his son.

The battleships, Scharnhorst and Gneisenau, each of 32,000 tons, were launched that year of 1936, at Wilhelmshaven and Kiel, within two months of each other and Gerhard wondered if he could be posted to one of them. The fitting-out and trials would take some eighteen months and he might be ready for, at least, a training cruise by then. It was all very exciting and thoughts of it almost overshadowed his regret at leaving Jelena. Also, early that year, the armoured ship, Admiral Graf Spee, was commissioned and it was in her, in 1937, that Gerhard, now a Seekadett, first went to sea, to the Coronation Review of King George VI and saw the might of the Royal Navy spread out - but few so modern as the pride of the Kriegsmarine. He wondered, as they lay at anchor off Portsmouth, if there would any chance of seeing Roddy. They had not met now for four years, since his birthday in the Summer of 1933 and Roddy was now a nineteen-year old Sub-lieutenant. Small likelihood of a meeting between him and a lowly Seekadett even if he were a member of the crew of the Kriegsmarine flagship. Gerhard listened to the Royal Marine Band playing on the quarter deck of the adjacent battleship and remembered his admiration of them on board his Uncle George's cruiser. He asked the junior lieutenant in charge of the little group of cadets if it would be possible to meet his cousin. That young man looked at him askance but said he would speak to a senior officer about shore leave. That was the last Gerhard heard of it - until a year later.

He and the other officer cadets had returned to the Naval Academy after their training cruise to England and he was now a midshipman, sporting a single gold star on his sleeves, indicating executive or line branch. Everything seemed to be going well with the meeting between Hitler and the 'British Prime Minister, ending with Chamberlain waving his 'bit of paper' as he left the aircraft and proclaiming 'Peace in our time,. Then, one of the college instructors called Gerhard into his office. He was the Political Officer and his message was unequivocal.

"If you want to progress, Metz" he said "I suggest you cast off your English connections. They didn't want you in the British Navy because you are half-German. Remember - if you want to rise in the Kriegsmarine, you must be wholly German."

It was a threat that had to be taken seriously. Gerhard

was about to write to Roddy to tell him that he could no longer have any contact when he realised the impossibility of explaining it without denigrating the regime that had imposed the ban. Since his letter was likely to be censored, if not withheld, he did not write it.

It was September. The 10,000 ton Prinz Eugen had been launched that summer and there was another heavy cruiser on the stocks, to be called Prinz Ludwig. Gerhard wondered if he would ever be appointed to one of them. Some of his fellows were being tempted by the visit of Günther Prien, already an ace, to enter the U-boat service but that held no attractions for Gerhard. Roddy, he had last heard of in HMS Hood, pride of the Royal Navy and Gerhard's aim was for the big ships, too. But they no longer corresponded so he did not hear that Roddy was now a junior watch keeper on board the cruiser HMS Bolton, paying a courtesy call to Hamburg that winter, the last winter of peace for six years.

Nor did Roddy know where 'Gair' was when he and two shipmates delved into a bierkeller in a fairly respectable district, having been threatened with dire retribution if they ventured to the Reeperbahn. Across the smoky, dim-lit room he could see a party of young officers of the Kriegsmarine who, while not rowdy, were singing student songs and naval ditties. A certain crystal clarity in the tenor leading them made him look more closely. Without doubt it was the cousin he had not seen for over five years.

His immediate impulse was to go over to them but the thought of the sudden stoppage of letters held him back. Was there a reason, a political reason, perhaps? He heard a change of song and recognized 'I had a Comrade' and looked across, wondering if it held a message. He knew no more of the words nor if they were apposite but he met Gerhard's eyes for a moment and knew what he tried to convey. The singers left soon after and as they passed the

British trio, Roddy attempted to show he understood by an infinitesimal nod.

This connection between the cousins, English and German, had gone unnoticed by Gerhard's party and by Roddy's two companions who only found that he had become rather quiet and introspective and put it down to the drink.

When Bolton left Hamburg, Roddy wrote to his father. He detailed the non-meeting and the conclusion he had drawn from it. He wondered if it might be better for 'Gair' if his English relations did not keep in touch. No doubt Jurgen would warn off his ex-wife, Gerhard's mother, if necessary.

The rumblings of war, like a distant train sending its vibrations ahead along the line, came nearer.

In August, the so-called pocket battleship, Graf Spee, sailed for the Atlantic and Gerhard Metz found himself a senior midshipman on board the Schleswig-Holstein. They were in the Baltic and he was able to snatch a brief twenty-four hours at the Königsberg house and to spend an hour or two with Jelena.

At dawn on the 1st. September Schleswig-Holstein opened the bombardment from the sea off the port of Danzig, German troops crossed the border with Poland and the war had begun. Two days later, Britain entered the fray.

It was a time of change for certain of the Trevane family. William and Robert, the two elder brothers were too old to get back to their former regiments. William and his Marchioness, bereft of most servants, retreated to the Dower House and turned their big house over to an evacuated girls' public school. Robert and Lucy took in some evacuees from Plymouth and put them in the servants' wing, turning the gardens over to vegetables. Lord George, the Vice Admiral was commanding a cruiser squadron in the Far East. Lady Anne became the first casualty when Harry Greville sent her home from India and her ship was torpedoed with few survivors.

Melanie, now seventeen, waited impatiently for admission into the WRNS, attainable at 17 1/2 . She was intensely emulative of her brother Roddy and, like him, had grieved at the loss of communication with their cousin.

"I wonder if he knows about Aunt Anne" she remarked to Roddy who was home for a brief forty-eight hours' leave from HMS Bolton.

"No reason why he should, I suppose" said Roddy. "Who would let him know? Unless Uncle Jurgen was informed - but why should he be?"

They contemplated the situation in silence for a while. Anne and Jurgen had been divorced for eleven years now and it seemed unlikely they had kept in touch after her re-marriage and their son's return to Germany.

Jurgen did know. The name of Lady Anne Greville in the list of lost passengers was seized upon and her marriage to and divorce from von Metz remarked on in the press together with her maiden status as a sister of the Marquis of Brent Haven. That she had a son was not mentioned but he was informed of her death in a letter from his father. He could not feel much more than a passing regret: she had not meant a great deal to him as a mother, since they had gone to Hayle and her rejection of him when she and Harry went to India had destroyed any lingering attachment. Cut off from his English connections and despising his stepmother, he had only his father to turn to. In effect, he was alone and the Navy was his mother and his father and his home.

Chapter 7

In the summer of 1940, Jurgen von Metz went to visit his property at Konigsberg. It was easier to reach now that the Polish Corridor was no longer in existence but he had always disliked it. Berlin winters were bad enough but East Prussian winters were abhorrent to him. He would have preferred to spend more time in Essen but Frederica did not care to leave Berlin: at least Anne had always been prepared to stay in Essen for as long as he wanted to be there.

There were still signs of Gerhard about in the Konigsberg house. He had seen little enough of his son and wondered at his choosing to spend most of his days here. To get away from Frederica was one reason, he knew. Frederica and her pride at capturing the top Nazis for her parties; still, it did his business no harm and his contracts to supply the war effort must be nearly equal to Krupps'.

It was here that he had met Frederica, daughter of a Polish Count and his half-Persian wife, both now dead. It was here that Jelena Krepka came to see him, heavily pregnant and told him she carried his grandchild. He listened to her, thoughtfully, gave her some money and said he would attend to the matter, dismissing her. Then he went to see the local gauleiter. He knew it was over ten months since Gerhard had been in Königsberg with his ship. He also knew the Krepkas were Jewish.

That done, he went to the jetty where Gerhard's boat rode at her moorings. He went aboard without haste, took a gun from his pocket and fired six shots into her bottom boards. Still without haste, he regained the jetty and watched the boat settle, gazing without expression until only her mast showed above the water. Then he walked back to the house.

The winter of '39-'40 had been bitter and the Polish snows had barely cleared. Jurgen was pleased to find a log fire blazing and called for mulled wine. Ridiculous in what was supposed to be summer. He recalled a long-ago visit to Anna's brother in Devon and the soft, warm air and the blue of sea and sky.

He should have had another child with Anna - Frederica was no brood mare - but his growing entanglement with the new National Socialist Workers' Party and then the stupid affair with the girl whom he could hardly remember now, had alienated her and led to the divorce. He had hardly expected her to go through with it: it did her no good so far as her standing and reputation were concerned. Men had these affairs which meant nothing and wives were not expected to take any notice. He had felt sufficient admiration and regret when she went ahead to let her take the boy for his childhood. Gerhard had come back so nothing had been lost there and was now a junior officer in the Kriegsmarine; a successful outcome.

The successful outcome, at that moment, was sprawled on the bunk in his cabin listening dreamily to a recording from a performance of Lohengrin, an aria featuring the great Lotte Blickman. She had a truly magnificent voice within that splendid figure upon the voluptuous bosom of which he had taken his early steps into manhood. His erotic memories were interrupted by the entry of a fellow junior leutnant bearing a vividly illustrated magazine.

"You ready, Gerdi?" he asked for although at present in harbour, they were due on duty shortly. Without waiting for an answer he thrust a picture in front of his colleague's face and said admiringly "Look at those!"

Gerhard looked at the picture of a heavy-bosomed Nordic blonde, leaning forward to display her charms supported in the newest form of brassiere, which she was advertising. Compared with Lotte's, they were grotesque.

"Bums in a hammock" grunted Gerhard and hauled himself off the bunk.

They were in Hamburg, it was Summer 1940 and at the Blohm & Voss shipyard the magnificent new battleship Bismarck was fitting-out and commissioning. They could see her superstructure from their own ship's berth and, coming on deck, both young leutnants looked across to her instinctively and both knew they harboured a desire to sail in her. Only one of them, however, was destined to be appointed to her.

In September, the great ship crept through the Kiel Canal to the Eastern Baltic, to Gotenhafen in Occupied Poland, to undergo sea trials, returning in December for the finishing touches at the Blohm & Voss yard. Gerhard was appointed to her, to join after Christmas leave.

He went to Berlin on Christmas Eve and left two days later to go to Königsberg. It was bitterly cold there and there was thick snow on the ground. He did not want to be there particularly but it was better than spending his leave in Berlin with Frederica, his father often absent and his stepmother too cloyingly affectionate. He changed from his uniform into thick winter clothing, a heavy jersey, a thick coat and a woollen hat and went out to go down to the shore, to the jetty where his little boat was tied.

The sight of the submerged wreck with just the pathetic

mast above the water shocked him into immobility. He wondered who could have done this, who would have done it and why they should have done it. He was staring into the water, at the shadowy outline of the boat, when something struck him on the back of the neck and he fell like a pole-axed ox.

He was not unconscious but sufficiently dazed to offer no resistance when he was pulled to his feet and propelled up to the road and into a car. There he collapsed on the back seat and closed his eyes against the dizziness that assailed him.

His captors were talking quietly amongst themselves - three of them, he reckoned as his brain began to function again - Polish partisans. He began to wonder what they wanted of him, how long they would keep him, if he would be free in time to take up his appointment to Bismarck.

Their destination was a rough camp in the woods and the man who received him, sitting on a tree stump by a blazing fire was Jerzy Krepka, a gaunt Jerzy with a growth of beard and a queer mixture of military and civilian clothing, a fur cap on his head.

"What are you doing here, Metz?" he said.

"Some leave before joining my ship" said Gerhard. "For God's sake, Jerzy, what is this? Why is my boat sunk? Why are you here?"

Jerzy stared at him for a few calculating moments.

"Your father sank your boat. Jelena was stupid enough to try to palm off her baby on you so he had her and our parents arrested and sent to a punishment camp and our home burned. I was out so I escaped them and came to join up with the group here. Do you tell me you did not know?"

"Of course not! But why arrested? For what? Why sink my boat?"

"Because we are Jews. So we could not get away in the

boat, I suppose. I don't know. I watched him sink it. Then, when I went home I saw the SS were there. So I hid."

Gerhard was silent for a long minute. The punishment camps - concentration camps - he did not know a lot about them.

"It was not my baby?" he said. .

"No, couldn't have been. She was seven months and you had not been here for ten."

The thought of that pliant and compliant body enduring the indignities, the tortures of a concentration camp rose in Gerhard's mind. He did not care to dwell on it. He looked around, at the wet, snow-spotted undergrowth, the fire of logs and twigs, the vigilant lookouts, armed, at a little distance from Jerzy, who was obviously their leader.

"Do you stay here, then?" he asked, for something to say.

"Not for long. We shift camps often. The soldiers search the woods every now and again so we don't make our presence too noticeable."

But what - what do you hope to do?"

Jerzy grinned.

"You don't expect me to answer that" he jeered.

"Well - what do you want with me? I cannot do anything about Jelena and your parents."

Jerzy shrugged.

"I just wanted you to know what your fine father has done to us. Because we are Jews - though he is married to one."

Gerhard stared. Frederica? Yet, somehow, now it had been said, he was not surprised.

"My stepmother is a Jewess" he said as if in confirmation.

"I wonder if he will have her sent to a camp" said Jerzy.

"I doubt if he knows. She claims a Persian grandmother" said Gerhard, slowly.

"I hope you will tell him." Jerzy stood up, a muffled, haggard figure and put out his hand. "I've no quarrel with you" he said. "We had good times and you treated me well. Go and join your fine ship and fight your hopeless war. Germany will not get away with this. Don't fear being killed because death will be better than life when you have lost again."

Gerhard took the proffered hand.

"Goodbye" he said. "Good luck."

They took him from the woods in the car and left him, once more, above the cold, grey Baltic and the jetty where his boat lay submerged. Jerzy's words were heavy in his mind. He was afraid of their truth.

He went to the house but it was bleak and cheerless and had no welcome for him now. He crouched before the log fire and wondered where Roddy was and what he was doing now. And Melanie?

Roddy was, in fact, the senior sub-lieutenant in HMS Bolton, ruling the Gun Room and the wide-eyed snotties with a rod of iron sheathed in velvet and hoping to achieve his second ring shortly which would probably mean a new posting. Melanie was a third officer WRNS, a cypher officer on the staff of C. in C. Western Approaches.

In his office in the Admiralty building, Vice Admiral Lord George Trevane knew where both his nephews were: a colleague in Naval Intelligence kept him up to date with the movements of his late sister's son and Roddy's promotion and subsequent posting to HMS Suffolk were in the bag. He was keeping track of Melanie's career, too.

Melanie, at that moment, was walking down the short drive of one of the houses in Mossley Hill that made up the WRNS Officers' Quarters, to get into the grey twelve-seated bus that took the watch keepers into Liverpool, to Derby House so far as she and her fellow watch mates were concerned. Once there, they descended into the Cypher office where they spent their time, day or night, under the harsh strip lighting. Watches were nominally four hours but at night they did a double one, combining the middle and morning watches so that they did not have to travel into Liverpool or back to Mossley Hill at around four a.m. because of the air-raids. If signal traffic was quiet, half the watch could usually sleep, in turn, in the wooden bunks underground - 'warm-bunking' where one rolled thankfully into the warm blankets just vacated by her relief.

Snow was falling the next morning as they came off watch and returned to Bruckley House for breakfast. As she walked down the hill afterwards, to her own quarters, Melanie glanced back. The snow flakes were falling softly, garbing the gaunt trees in white, carpeting the road. The sheer beauty of it made her stop, gazing. Other girls, hurrying from the Mess at Bruckley House to get to their cabins in the scattered houses, gathered her up with them and she went, ready to bath and turn in to sleep until lunchtime. The peace and serenity of the scene stayed with her until a day or two later when ugly reality broke into it.

The snow had become blackened slush when she went along to a small drinks party at one of the other houses. One of the guests in a group was a rather Gung-ho Army officer who had either imbibed unwisely or had a job beyond his capabilities which made him shoot off his mouth.

"Quite happy with the simple life" he declared, his rather blood-shot gaze lingering on Melanie's slender figure and dark hair and eyes. "Like that French general in the last lot who said all he needed was a good horse to ride, a war to fight and a woman to bed. Neat, eh?" The invitation to Melanie was unmistakeable.

"I think, since his time, women have found better things in life to do" she said, coolly. "I doubt if-you'll find many horses in Liverpool so you'll just have to fight your war."

She found the senior officer in those Quarters, made her thanks and farewells and got her coat and hat. On the way to her own house she was caught by another erstwhile guest, a young RNVR lieutenant.

"I say" he said. "Are you off duty tonight? Shall we go into Liverpool?"

Melanie stopped at the gate of her house.

"I am not looking to bed with anyone" she said.

"Oh, come on" he said. "I'm back to sea tomorrow. I might be killed."

She was angry.

"In that case you'd never know if you'd got a child on the poor fool who gratified you" she snapped. "It's a long time now since women realised they're not here just to pleasure men. Grow up, laddie." She left him at the gate and went indoors, angry at herself for giving way to her anger and also at the attitude of the two males.

Chapter 8

When Gerhard Metz, a junior leutnant in Bismarck, realised that HMS Hood was amongst the British ships pursuing Bismarck and Prinz Eugen, he wondered if Roddy was still with her. That Roddy was actually in one of the other pursuing ships, HMS Suffolk, he could not know. The abrupt destruction of the great Hood appalled both sides. Even so, the fact that the newly commissioned and sorely-damaged Prince of Wales was not finished off raised many questions also on both sides.

As a trainee watch keeper with duties on the bridge, Gerhard had plenty of opportunity to observe the very different characters of the frail Commander of Bismarck, Kapitän zur See Lindemann and the Admiral in charge of the two ships, Lütjens. Lindemann would have continued the battle but Lütjens, fearfully conscious of Hitler's orders that their mission was to destroy merchant shipping carrying supplies to Britain and not to engage with British warships, broke off the fight, sending Prinz Eugen on to the Atlantic convoy routes and Bismarck to make for Brest.

The bad weather, the intense cold and the fact that Lütjens kept everybody at action stations meant that no-one went to bed for night after night but sought what sleep they could on the deck, crouched by the guns, in a corner of the chartroom, wherever there was a space with some sort of shelter from the cold and wet.

Gerhard, in a haze of exhaustion, scurrying from one job to another, hardly knew by what they were attacked. Sometimes from the sea, sometimes from the air and then, at last, as he paused to take breath, the bomb that landed close astern and jammed the rudder hard over so that they set off on an eternal circle.

On the last morning he went to the bridge, sent by the fourth gunnery officer to try to find out the current situation. He saw the Captain, sitting with his breakfast and knew that he had given up the command of his proud ship and would not survive her loss nor the loss of his honour.

Some said that both Lütjens and Lindemann were killed by a shell destroying the bridge but other survivors said they had seen the Captain step off his ship as she went down and sink with her. In the last desperate moments, Gerhard found himself urging some sailors to look out for themselves, to jump overboard, to make for one of the drifting floats or life-rafts, sure that the British ships would pick up all they could. He did not remember much after that until he found himself with two others on a raft and saw that the British ships, warned of the approach of U-boats, were making off, leaving hundreds of survivors still in the sea.

Two days later he was picked up by a U-boat. His companions were dead. The U-boat landed him at Lorient and he was taken to the military hospital where he lay in bed, barely conscious, his mind still full of the sound of battle, the sight of fire, twisted metal, mutilated bodies, struggling men fighting their way up to the decks, the tortured ship rolling over, the bobbing heads amongst the oil and debris on the water, the raft and the cold, always the cold and the desperate weariness.

But his youth and the good food - casualties from U-boats were taken to this hospital and Dönitz saw to it that his U-boat crews were well fed - prevailed and he came to terms with his experiences and, at last, was put on the train for Germany for his survivor's leave, a hardened, stern-faced young man with plenty of pay in his pocket and a determination to use his leave to the full.

However, the pleasures of the flesh failed to satisfy, he was still too close to the ship and his vanished colleagues. Should go back to sea at once, he decided morosely, as an airman after a crash or a horseman after a fall. In one cellar bar he remembered the brief meeting of eyes with Roddy and a wave of nostalgia swept over him, memories of the house in Devon and the river and Roddy and Melanie. But, perhaps Roddy had vanished too, in Hood, to lie forever under the waves with his lost colleagues.

In Berlin, he found his father was in Essen. The valet, Strauss, had gone with him but Emil and Paul were still there, too old now for call-up to the Forces. July in Berlin, hot and smelly, the linden trees in full leaf, the streets full of Brown shirted SA, Army officers still exercising in the Park - it was said Admiral Canaris rode there too - sitting their horses with casual ease. Gerhard thought of the days out hunting with Roddy and Melanie and his mother. He had not thought of his mother, consciously, for a long time now, not since she had deserted him for Harry Greville and put him on board the old freighter Longbow with the kindly Captain Bone and gone off to India. He had heard that Longbow had been in a convoy from Halifax and among the ships sunk by a U-boat pack but he hoped that Captain Bone would have retired by then. He had no way of knowing that the seventy-year old skipper and the seventy-year old retired Admiral, Commodore of the convoy, had gone down together in the equally old freighter with all her crew and the vital supplies she was carrying in her holds and on her deck.

Frederica von Metz was missing her husband's bedtime attentions. She watched her stepson one evening after dinner, recognizing his unrest as he lounged on a sofa, leafing through a magazine, a glass of gin to hand and speculated on his prowess. He was no longer a boy; he had returned from the hospital in all respects a man.

"How do you occupy yourselves in the evening on your ship?" she enquired tentatively.

"In port or at sea?" he said. "On duty or off?"

"Off duty - in port" she suggested.

He put down the magazine and gave her a fairly crude description of a night in port.

"We drove back to the docks in one of the fellows' car and a line of matelots at the side of the road all saluted us - with a shower of piss all over the car. Fortunately it rained..."

"Why are men such disgusting, dirty little schoolboys when they get together?" she wondered, visualizing the line of upraised penises along the side of the road. "I suppose they'd all been to the local brothels. Do you find you benefited from Lotte's tuition?"

He concealed his astonishment and found he was annoyed that she had known about his initiation.

"Shall we find out?" he said. "Perhaps you can improve on her."

She thought, with a quickening excitement, perhaps she could. With this slim, taut body, after Jurgen's thickening figure and heavy limbs, who knew to what heights they could rise? She stood up and put out her hand to him.

"Go" he said. "I will join you." He took up his drink.

Frederica went, slightly subdued. So he was not to be led, a willing lamb, to be fondled and undressed but would come to her while she awaited his pleasure, in bed.

Lying there, she decided he was right. She was still slim and not ashamed of her body but she was, well, over forty and, at least, in bed in a delicate nightdress could conceal any slight deficiency in her figure.

He took her with an efficient thoroughness that at first frightened her and then brought her to writhing and crying, satiated yet striving for more, collapsing exhausted when, ruthless, he aroused her and took her again. Then he left her, whimpering in her bed, in a haze of repletion.

He went, the next morning, to find an acquaintance at the Marineamt, in Personnel, to see if he could get an immediate posting. The officer, with the three rings of a korvetten-kapitän, regarded him thoughtfully.

"A Bismarck survivor, Metz?" he said.

"Yes." Gerhard touched the Iron Cross on his reefer. "For which I got this - though God knows I did nothing but be thoroughly scared."

"You did your job, you directed others off the ship, you endured two days on a raft, you spent some weeks in hospital." The Personnel officer looked up from the open folder on his desk. "Why don't you want to finish your leave?"

"I want to be back in a ship. I find all this superficial." The gesture of his arm encompassed the whole of Berlin beyond the building. "I don't want nightclubs and brothels. I've even fucked my stepmother."

The korvetten-kapitän smothered a smile.

"They say experience of an older woman is good for a young man" he conceded. "So you want to go to sea? I can tell you that you were in line for a shore posting with Navy Group West; but you'd prefer to be in a destroyer? Or a cruiser?"

"I have a choice?"

"Prinz Eugen is in Brest with Scharnhorst and Gneisenau. We're sending another batch of cadets there to join them. If you can leave immediately you can go down in charge of them. All right?"

When Gerhard got back to the house he found his father had returned. Frederica was not in sight. He went to his room to pack his kit - all new, replacing that which had gone down in Bismarck. He had a feeling of hatred: he hated Berlin and this house and his father. He hated his stepmother and what she was and what they had done. He wanted to hurt, to be back in battle, to be spewing out shells at the enemy. He did not recognize it as a consequence of his own hurt.

He sent for Paul to carry his bags down and to ring for a cab to take him to the station. Then he went to his father.

"An early recall?" said Jurgen. "You had more leave, surely?"

"I asked for a new posting. I need to get back to a ship." Gerhard paused and added "Last night I screwed Frederica." He observed the shock and dawning fury on Jurgen's face with detachment and, as his father came towards him with hand upraised, went on "I wondered if it would be any different with a Jewess."

It stopped Jurgen as if he had come up against a solid wall. He whispered breathlessly "What did you say?"

"You know what I said." Gerhard turned to go. "Your marriage is illegal."

Chapter 9

The midshipmen sent to Brest were quartered at first 'tween decks in the two great ships but British bombers inflicted so much damage and so many casualties that they were removed to quarters fifteen miles away. Each morning they piled into lorries to return to work on the ships and each evening they took to the lorries for the journey back to their quarters.

Gerhard Metz stayed with them for six months. It was a strange time for him. He felt that something in him had died with his mates in Bismarck; and he did not know what he had done to his father and to Frederica. He had no letters from them. Then he went back to Berlin on Christmas leave.

December had been a good month so far - and in the previous month the British ships Ark Royal and Barham had been sunk in the Mediterranean. Now Japan had attacked the American fleet in Pearl Harbour and Germany and Italy had declared war on the U.S. The Repulse and the Prince of Wales had been sunk off the Malay Peninsula and Valiant and Queen Elizabeth were crippled at Alexandria. Gerhard had reason to feel the war was progressing in their favour but it gave him no great pleasure.

Only Emil and Paul and the cook were in the house.

Jurgen, it seemed, spent more time now in Essen. Emil eventually confided in hushed tones that Frederica was in Ravensbrück concentration camp for women, it having been discovered that she had concealed the fact that her mother was a Jewess and not, as she had said, the daughter of a Persian woman.

Gerhard accepted the news in silence. He had disliked his stepmother but had she deserved this? But his father had done it to the Krepka family - had Jelena deserved it either? He ate his Christmas dinner alone and thought of the Christmas at Hayle when his mother and Nanny Stanton had let him and Melanie have their milk and biscuits in their dressing gowns in front of the log fire by the Christmas tree and Anne, the following day, had taken them to the Meet when they had followed hounds for an hour and a half before... He broke off his thoughts, wishing he had news of Roddy, alive or in the wreckage of Hood.

Lieutenant Roderick Trevane, RN., was wishing much the same of 'Gair' - that he had news of him - and the day before the New Year of 1942 dawned, he was walking towards the Admiralty buildings with the hope that his uncle, Admiral Lord George, might be able to inform him.

The bombing of London had eased but the damage was widespread and unescapable. Lord George had his office in the underground HQ now and the ground level entrances were piled high with sandbags. Roddy was led by a messenger through a maze of grey depressing passages.

Uncle George, Roddy thought when he was admitted to the presence, was looking rather worn. Of course, he must be around sixty now and had lived a full and active service life. He greeted his nephew in a kindly fashion and waved him to a chair. "Family call, Roderick?" he said "Or looking for a new appointment?" He knew full well where Roddy's next commission was to be.

"Family call, sir, before I join my new ship."

The Admiral nodded, smiling tiredly.

"Number One in a corvette" he confirmed. "It won't be easy, Rod."

"No, sir. Have you news of Melanie?"

"She's still with C. in C. W.A."

"And - our cousin on the other side?"

"I've not heard anything of him for sometime. He was in Brest with Scharnhorst some months ago. I have a feeling they should be making a break for it, soon."

"Home - or into the Atlantic?"

"Suit us if they went home. We could contain them better in the North Sea than in the Atlantic."

The following month the two battle cruisers, Scharnhorst and Gneisenau, obliged together with the heavy cruiser Prinz Eugen and made a run for it from Brest, through the English Channel, hugging the French coast to take advantage of air cover and getting home despite being damaged twice by mines. Air attack by British 'planes was sadly mismanaged and resulted in unnecessary losses.

At that time Gerhard Metz had taken up his deferred posting to Navy Group West and was busy enough at his desk job. Working at Headquarters, even a desk job, had compensations. A young, single, not unhandsome officer was rarely short of entertainment or companionship. For a while Gerhard threw himself into the lifestyle enjoyed by his peers. But it didn't last. As the year dragged on through Summer he became increasingly restless. Three years of war, he had now been through. His mind turned frequently to his years in England, to Roddy and Melanie. He did not want to be fighting them. He wished to know that they were safe, that the bombing by the Luftwaffe had not affected them. He could not bear to think of Roddy's ship being a prey to the U-boats, concentrated in the North Atlantic since July. He went on Christmas leave and stared at the devastation as the train left France and made its way across Germany. In Berlin he was brought up sharply by a long column of drably garbed people, old men, women and children, lined up outside a station from which trains left for the East, where he had caught trains to go to Königsberg. Jews, he thought and as he realised it, his eye was caught by a tall woman who clutched a bedraggled fur coat about her thin figure. Frederica.

"Where are they going?" he asked a passer-by.

"Poland" said the man. "They are being re-settled in Poland."

Gerhard nodded his thanks and understanding. Poland. Well, at least, that was where she had come from. But - re-settled? What sort of re-settlement? A punishment camp, a concentration camp like the Krepkas? His father had done that. Did that excuse what he had done to Frederica?

He made his way to the Metz house where Paul told him that his father was in Berlin but was at present with the Fuhrer discussing production figures. That Jurgen should be there, closeted with Hitler, while his ex-wife stood in a line of deportees not far away made Gerhard feel slightly nauseated. Had Frederica deserved that? Had the Krepkas? Did the Jews present such a threat to Europe that they must be exterminated? He could hardly envisage Jerzy or Jelena as a threat: until now with Jerzy driven from his home, leading a group of partizans which might well become a threat to the occupying troops.

When his father returned and Paul had served them with coffee and cakes, Gerhard remarked that he had seen Frederica. Jurgen paused a moment before asking casually where he had seen her.

"Near the station - before transported to Poland."

Jurgen finished his cake.

"Bitch" he said. "Persian grandmother indeed."

"Where will they go in Poland?" asked Gerhard.

"Camps" said Jurgen, tersely. "For displaced persons.

Krupps are taking on some workers from a camp near Essen. I might - cheap labour."

Gerhard went to Essen with his father for the rest of his leave. It was on his way to Navy Group West anyway and in wartime one never knew if there would be another time. But there he saw the slave workers being herded into the great Krupps works, thin, raggedly clothed in the bitter weather and wondered if all pity, all compassion had gone. Had it always been so or was it because, deep down everyone knew they were fighting a war already lost - lost from the moment Hitler declared war on America. In the Navy, he thought, there is still some honour and feeling left: he remembered rescued seamen of both sides. Then, also, he remembered those left to drown.

In the New Year he was appointed to the cruiser Graf Lückner, due to sail for the Atlantic as a commerce raider. Her Captain was also newly joined and the ship's company were waiting to take the measure of their new CO. He was a slight, quiet man, worthy of his appointment and had a care for the welfare of his young crew and expected his officers to care for them too. Kapitän zur See Lucien Falke also endeavoured to follow the example of his predecessor in Graf Spee in causing minimal casualties among the crews of the ships upon which he preyed. Merchant seamen were not looked on as combatants and it seemed to be most unfair that they ceased to be employed and therefore had no pay when they left a ship - or the ship left them. In other words, their pay was stopped at the moment their ship was destroyed.

Apart from their depredations on merchant shipping, a major part of the role of a commerce raider was to disrupt the movements of the enemy's warships. So Falke spread his activities fairly widely across the North and South Atlantic and the Indian Ocean. As one of his watch-keeping officers, Gerhard Metz learned a great deal about the leadership of men and also re-discovered the meaning of pity and compassion. This came about as they were homeward bound in May, having been relieved by another surface raider. They were not to find themselves in such a battle as had brought about the end of Spee's activities and were happily looking forward to a spell of leave, ignoring the fact that their path had recently been crossed by a convoy on its way back from Murmansk. The convoy's escort commander, however, despatched one of his cruisers, HMS Bolton, to investigate the ship supposedly treading on his tail.

Orders from Hitler were that his surface ships avoided contact with British warships whenever possible but when challenged by Bolton with her battle ensigns hoisted there was no choice.

But Lückner had the advantage in firepower and also in luck. A broadside from her demolished Bolton's bridge and fighting top and within ninety minutes she was ablaze, little more than a floating hulk with the greater part of her crew wounded, dead or dying. Falke and his officers watched through their glasses as the British seamen brought up wounded to lie on her quarter-deck and fought the flames with hoses. Falke had ordered a cease fire although Bolton's battle ensigns still fluttered defiantly.

It was then that the strange lull in the weather came; the wind died, the sea became like glass. Falke spoke of it wonderingly after the war when the British commended him for his rescue of one hundred and twenty survivors of the crippled ship which he effected by laying Graf Lückner alongside Bolton and transferring them from deck to deck. Among them were the only two remaining officers, the CO, Captain Mitchell and Lieutenant Carter, dying with shrapnel in his spine. There were others who died and British and German sailors together were committed to the deep and the surviving British sang 'Eternal Father, Strong to Save'. There were tears in many eyes and Gerhard could believe again that humanity prevailed in even the most bitter circumstances.

Chapter 10

Melanie looked at her brother and accepted regretfully that the war was taking its toll. His corvette had gone straight from Atlantic escort duties to assisting in the Normandy landings and he was now on a week's leave. She was on a forty-eight hour break, changing jobs. After an uncertain June the sun was shining and they were lying on the grass by the river.

She was in two minds about her new posting. While in Western Approaches Command she could keep an eye on Roddy's ship and their comings and goings on convoys as he was also in Western Approaches.

"I'm not going back to Liverpool" she told him. "I'm going to London. I shall be with Uncle George."

"I'm not going back to Liverpool, either" he said. "I've been given a destroyer - in command - and a half-stripe."

Something in his voice checked her congratulations.

"Pleased?" she said, after a moment's pause.

"Yes" he said, with a sigh. "Mel, you do realise that if anything happens to me, this place will be yours? You will inherit."

It would be stupid to say nothing will happen to you. A destroyer - where? Equally, a bomb in London. Who knew what might happen to either of them. One did not think about it, ordinarily. But, of course, one knew fear in an air raid as, no doubt, Roddy knew fear during U-boat attacks - or was he too busy at the time to feel anything but the immediate demands on him?

She shrugged.

"Che sera" she said. Roddy rolled over on to his back.

"One of our fellows came back from leave - just got married" he said and she recognized that he was leaving the question of their future. "He had let his bride wash and iron his bell bottoms and she'd pressed them with fore and aft creases instead of the regulation seven horizontal and he hadn't time to re-do them before catching his train."

"What happened?" she enquired, amused.

"Oh, he got put on a charge - improperly dressed - but I think Jimmy let him off when he pleaded his wife was new and didn't know any better."

She tried to laugh and to sustain a lighter mood but it was no good. They got up and, with linked arms, strolled back to the house to have tea with their parents. They could not know that it would be the last time they would be together.

Melanie left for London and the Admiralty the next morning to take up her new post. Roddy had half the week before taking up his new command. He was restless and did not know how to fill the time. The evacuees had long since returned to their homes in Plymouth and Robert and Lucy helped the solitary and ancient gardener in growing and gathering vegetables, most of which went to the village shop. Robert was nominally in charge of the Home Guard but the thought of invasion was past and they had mainly to look out for the odd survivors from shot-down 'planes or for any possible person acting suspiciously who could be labelled spy. Most of the glass had gone from the greenhouses but Lucy regularly put on her green tweed costume, maroon blouse and pork-pie hat and took what fruit she could to the hospital where, in turn with other members of the WVS she pushed a library trolley round the wards. They were all war-weary and accepted the on-going news of the Normandy landings without great excitement. The foothold was gained but they knew that a long slog and many casualties lay ahead.

Gerhard Metz had by now joined the commerce raider, a heavy cruiser called Prinz Ludwig. Her Captain was a younger man than Falke of the Graf Luckner, a very different character in some aspects. Lean, thin-faced and tautly-strung, he had been described as a 'live wire' and. a 'bright spark'. His father had owned a shipping line and when the crews were taken to man the U-boats in 1917, he had sent his twelve-year-old son to sea as a cadet. The boy had learned hard yet his experiences had made him both understanding and compassionate with the gift of leadership which Gerhard took in and hoped passionately to be able to emulate. Roddy, he thought, would have it, part of his inheritance, his upbringing. Perhaps, through his mother, he would have the makings of it too, the inbred habit of command of the British aristocracy. He did not often, now, think, of his mixed parentage but as he stood. on Prinz Ludwig's bridge he did wonder where he would be if Dartmouth had accepted him. Certainly not watching Kapitän zur See Dettner and Fregattan-Kapitän Kassel Zeiss glasses to their eyes, waiting to see if the thin plumes of smoke, heralded by a look-out, would turn out to be the expected liner, SS Curie, travelling alone and not in convoy because of her speed and carrying Canadian troops and flyers to join the invasion of Europe.

The liner, pursuing her course towards the Azores - following the Gulf Stream because it was said the waters were too warm for the U-boats - had come into range and Prinz Ludwig, possibly still beyond her sight, opened up with her formidable broadside and straddled the troopship with the first salvo. The second struck the bridge and started a fire on the foredeck. It was not long before she was a burning, sinking wreck and the sea was dotted with hundreds of bobbing heads and waving arms as the raider drew nearer. Gerhard noted some of their crew gathering near the lifeboats, ready to launch a rescue attempt. But the troopship had got off a radio message 'Am being attacked by a surface raider' and given their position. Dettner let his glasses drop to his chest and gave the order All engines full ahead and they left the scene swiftly, not knowing how near other ships might be. At first, Gerhard felt horrified protest; then he saw his Captain's eyes, saw him pass the back of his hand across his lips and understood the price of command.

Gerhard's own command and promotion to Kapitän-leutnant came at the beginning of 1945, a destroyer and he had been CO for some two months when, about 400 km. West of Bergen, they met the enemy ship.

Roddy had been in command for about eight months and reckoned to be some 250 miles East of the Shetlands when his look-outs spotted the enemy destroyer.

The damaged ship ploughed on doggedly, though at reduced speed, headed hopefully towards her home port; the fire on the foredeck was out and most of the holes patched. The duty watch were still at defence stations and waiting for the cover of darkness when out of the twilight came three bombers, possibly on their way home from a sortie on land, possibly jettisoning their load. One bomb hit the foredeck again and went through to the forecastle where the watch below were grabbing sandwiches and tea. The second hit the bridge just as the CO, rushing up from the sickbay, reached it. A third shattered the only remaining gun. Between them, they put paid to the two remaining boats and scattered the life rafts. The stricken ship came to a stop, wallowing helplessly, alone again on the sea.

The few able-bodied men left, under the direction of a bloodied midshipman, set about what damage control was possible. The forepart of the ship was ablaze and though they might bring the fire within bounds again, the rescue of men in the mess decks below was not likely. The wounded were brought up from the sickbay and down from the wrecked bridge and laid out on the quarter deck. That any of them could survive in the cold Northern waters was improbable.

The only remaining officer, feeling lightheaded from loss of blood, cast a despairing look round, wondering if it were really worth-while to try to get the wounded on to rafts and floats. On the quarter-deck he saw the two COs had been laid side by side; he had heard that they were cousins and briefly contemplated the fate that had brought them together like this. Then his weakness overcame him and he sank to the deck, almost gratefully surrendering the responsibility that had descended upon his eighteen-year old shoulders. The senior rating left, a grizzled petty officer, grimly assumed it and directed those still active to get the rafts overboard and get themselves and the wounded on to them. Somehow, he could not leave them on deck to go down with the ship and the already dead.

Roddy, finding himself on a bobbing float with Gerhard and the midshipman, with others clinging around it, looked into his cousin's eyes and clasped his hand.

"I wish" said Gerhard "They had taken me at Dartmouth. How's Melanie?"

"She's well. With Uncle George."

"Good. "

They were silent awhile. Beside them, the teenager gave up his short life and another took his place while he floated away quietly with the other bodies in the grey sea.

"Gair" said Roddy, his voice fading. "Can you sing?"

Gerhard did not answer. But a moment later the crystal

clear notes rose into the darkening sky.

'Abide with me, fast falls the eventide

'The darkness deepens, Lord with me abide"

A few voices, a few humming, joined in. Roddy tried but could not recall the words.

*Where is death's sting, Where, grave, thy Victory?"

It was so cold and the last light had gone. Roddy remembered his home and the last days with Melanie when he had told her that she would inherit if he were killed. As in a dream he heard the last verse.

'Hold thou thy Cross before my closing eyes'

but when Heaven's morning broke, the ship that found the wreckage found only the dead. Because the ship was not heading for home but was going to the Denmark Strait, the bodies that were picked up were given a burial at sea.

Melanie, coming on watch, was called to Admiral Trevane's office. She knew immediately on seeing his face that he had grave news for her.

"Roddy?" she said, involuntarily.

"Yes. Both" he said, heavily. "Roddy and Gerhard. Together."

The Signals Officer, watching from a discreet distance as Admiral and Second Officer had a brief embrace, enlightened the Staff Captain.

"His two nephews. Her brother and cousin."

"You'd better take forty-eight hours' leave and go home to your parents" said Lord George. "They won't know, yet."

Tell them before the telegram arrives, thought Melanie and the announcement on the wireless 'The Admiralty regrets to announce the loss of HMS - ." Would they also announce the loss of the other? 'With no survivors.'

It was too early for the roses that had been blooming when she and Roddy were last at home. 'No roses grow on a sailor's grave.' She walked from the office.